THE McVENTURES OF ME, MORGAN McFACTOID

THE McVENTURES OF ME, MORGAN McFACTOID

HAIR TODAY, GONE TOMORROW

MARK S. WAXMAN

Sky Pony Press
New York

Sky Pony Press books may be purchased in bulk at special discounts for sales promotion, corporate gifts, fundraising, or educational purposes. Special editions can also be created to specifications. For details, contact the Special Sales Department, Sky Pony Press, 307 West 36th Street, 11th Floor, New York, NY 10018 or info@skyhorsepublishing.com.

Sky Pony® is a registered trademark of Skyhorse Publishing, Inc.®, a Delaware corporation.

Visit our website at www.skyponypress.com.

10 9 8 7 6 5 4 3 2 1

Manufactured in the United States of America

Library of Congress Cataloging-in-Publication Data is available on file.

Cover design & illustrations by Sarah Brody

Print ISBN: 978-1634501484
Ebook ISBN: 978-1-63450-955-8

To Paula, David, and Taylor

TABLE OF CONTENTS

CHASED BY A BRONTOSAURUS

By the time you finish reading this sentence, ninety-three babies will have been born in the world, thirty-two thousand tons of water will have splashed over Niagara Falls, the earth will have rotated fifty-eight miles to the left at a speed twenty times faster than a bullet fired out of a rifle, and you'll have learned three very cool facts!

By the time you finish reading this page, more than 1.4 million video clips will have been watched on YouTube.

And by the time you finish reading this book, you'll learn that I was offered *billions* of dollars (counting to one billion nonstop, day and night, would take thirty-two years) for a monumental invention I came up with—an invention that almost got me killed. (The word "almost" is the longest word in the English language with all the letters in alphabetical order.)

By the time he was eight years old, Mozart had composed his first symphony. I just turned thirteen and I still haven't learned how to whistle, but soon everybody will know my name, which, by the way, is Morgan McCracken.

Not everyone calls me Morgan, though.

My grandfather, Poppy, calls me Sparky, because he thinks I have an "imaginative spark." My irritating sister calls me Mister McFactoid, because I'm always spouting freaky facts and weird trivia. And the kids at school call me all kinds of names, probably because I'm different.

I look different—I have unruly red hair and 203 freckles on my face.

I think different—I wonder about things like, how do you handcuff a one-armed man? And who was the first person to look at a cow and say, "I think I'll squeeze these dangly things and drink whatever comes out?" And why is "bra" singular but "panties" plural?

And I act different—I'm an inventor. I invent strange things that usually get me into trouble and sometimes get me back out of trouble. For example, my *Spring-Loaded Shoes* allow me to jump a six-foot fence in a single, spectacular leap. And my *Have A Seat Pants* are trousers that turn into chairs, so you can always sit down when you want to. And I'm working on a device that would record dreams so you could watch them later.

Unfortunately, I hadn't invented anything to save me from Brad Buckholtz Jr., the meanest kid in school, who had decided one particular day would be my last particular day on earth. I wished I had devised a way for a person to instantly disappear, to evaporate, to vanish in a flash. Because that's what I needed to do that afternoon. Brad hated me and he was determined to pound my red-freckled face into a bloody, red pulp. Neither one of us had any idea that our chilling encounter would lead to my billion-dollar idea.

It all started after school, when nothing good ever happens. I was alone in the science room eating my favorite snack (french fries) and finishing my water displacement project. I was proving why an aircraft carrier floats, but a carpenter nail sinks. (McDonald's uses about 7 percent of the potatoes grown in the United States for its french fries. And an aircraft carrier is longer than the Empire State Building.)

I heard the classroom door squeak open and a nasal voice say, "Hello, Hairy." It was the monster, Brad Buckholtz Jr. My heart started to beat faster. My blood went cold. Buckholtz, who had failed to graduate the eighth grade (three times!), was walking toward me along with his idiot friends, the short and fat Jerry the Jerk and the tall and thin Donald the Dope. Side by side, they looked like a ball and bat. I tried to ignore Buckholtz, but he spat on my plastic model aircraft carrier. A thick, booger-green loogie dripped from the flight deck. Brad's kiss-up friends cracked up.

"Hello, Brad," I said, trying to keep my voice from shaking.

"Hairy, Hairy, Hairy," he replied.

"You can call me Morgan . . . Morgan, Morgan."

"Are you making fun of me?"

Here's the deal: He liked to call me "Hairy" because I was the only boy in middle school with facial hair. I mean, I didn't look like Santa Claus or Yosemite Sam. I just had some stubble. Buckholtz, whose face was as smooth (and as attractive) as a bowling ball, was envious that I shaved like a man. At almost sixteen years old, he still didn't have a single hair on his chin—not even peach fuzz on his cheeks. It pissed him off. And he took his anger out on me.

Buckholtz and his bozos weren't the only ones who kidded me about my looks. Since moving from Boston, Massachusetts, to Carlsbad, California, six months earlier, the students at my new school had pointed at my red hair, my red freckles, and the red stubble on my chin—and called me everything from "Carrot Top" to "Measles Man" to "Moss Mug."

Buckholtz helped himself to my french fries. "We could smell these from down the hall. I just had to have one."

"Have two," I said.

"Ow ode r u, Hairy?" he mumbled, his big mouth full of fries.

"How *odd* am I?"

He swallowed the fries and asked his question again, louder. "How *old* are you? Everyone already knows how odd you are."

"Thirteen."

"No, really. How old are you?"

I don't believe in violence. But right then, I wished I were seven feet tall with massive muscles and gigantic fists of granite. Then I could "Picasso" him with one powerful punch—you know, rearrange his face so he'd see with his ears, smell with his eyes, and chew french fries in his nose.

"Your mommy must be feeding you special vitamins or something," Buckholtz said as he munched more of my fries. Jerry and Donald finished the rest.

"She's not," I said.

"Then why do you have hair on your face? Huh, Hairy, why?"

"I don't know. And my name is Morgan."

"Maybe, Hairy Face, your name is 'Werewolf,'" Buckholtz said, taking a step toward me. Jerry snickered. Donald giggled.

"Yeah, maybe he's a werewolf," Jerry said, elbowing Donald deep in the ribs.

While they were busy guffawing way too much, I sneaked a small plastic packet of ketchup into my hand and popped it into my mouth. I turned to them. "I *am* a werewolf!" I roared, tilting my head back and widening my eyes. Buckholtz's friends stopped laughing. All you could hear was the ticking of the classroom clock. "My hair used to be blond," I said, moving toward the classroom door.

"What's that supposed to mean?" Buckholtz snapped.

"I've sucked so much blood that my hair turned red!" (For the record, werewolves are not bloodsucking vampires, but I figured these three imbeciles wouldn't know the difference.) I bit down hard on the ketchup packet and out spurted red gobs between my teeth.

Brad laughed.

Jerry the Jerk laughed.

But Donald the Dope apparently couldn't stomach the sight of blood. Even fake blood. He gagged a couple of times, grabbed his stomach, and hurled.

All over Brad's boots.

His *new* boots.

"Uh oh. Your dad's gonna *kill* you!" Jerry the Jerk said to Brad.

Buckholtz looked down at the barf on his boots, then he slowly looked up at me. "You're gonna lick these boots clean. And I'm gonna clean your face, one little hairy nub at a time." His fat hand swiped a pair of tweezers off the lab counter and he started toward me, but he slipped and fell in the puddle of fresh puke. His favorite T. rex T-shirt was splattered with chunks of Donald's lunch and undigested french fries. That made him crazy mad. He yelled, "You're dead! You can kiss your hairy face goodbye!"

THE GODDESS ACROSS THE STREET

I ran to the door, shoved it open, and sprinted down the empty hall. One of my sneakers fell off, so I ran with a limp.

It wasn't the first time Buckholtz had chased me and it wouldn't be the last. Unless he caught me. Then chances were, it *would* be the last, because Brad Buckholtz was strong and evil. He once wanted to get his hands on a pigeon's nest resting on a high branch, so he yanked the small tree out of the ground, roots and all. *That* sort of strong. Then he stepped on the pigeon eggs. *That* kind of evil.

And he weighed as much as a bulldozer. I swear the floor shook as he lumbered down the hall after me. But as big as he was, he was fast. (A three-ton African elephant can run twenty-five miles per hour. That's three times faster than a house mouse.)

I avoided his grasp outside the cafeteria, then I ran toward the baseball field, dived under the fence behind center field, and darted down the alley next to our school. I wish I had worn my *Spring-Loaded Shoes* that day. Maybe Buckholtz's belly couldn't fit under the fence or possibly he chose to let me live one more day, but whatever the reason, when I turned around Buckholtz was no longer on my tail. Even so, I didn't take any chances. I kept running. As Poppy says, *"It's better to be a coward for a minute than dead for the rest of your life."*

I sped past kids walking home from school. (In the average lifetime, a person will walk the equivalent of five times around the equator.) They ignored me, chatting, no doubt, about who was going with whom to the Valentine's Day dance. They were totally unaware that Buckholtz had sworn to throw me to the ground and pluck every single hair out of my face, one whisker at a time. And then, kill me.

I had never run harder or farther with one shoe or two. I used every shortcut I could think of to get to my house. I climbed over old lady Dewberry's brick wall and dropped into her backyard, ripping my jeans and exposing my underpants (the striped ones . . . with a hole in them).

Fortunately, Dewberry's Rottweiler was locked in the house, barking and scratching at the sliding glass door. Dewberry stood in her well-kept flowerbed, seething and shaking a trowel at me. Unlike her dog, Dewberry had no front teeth. Like her dog, she had foam dribbling from her bottom lip.

"Get off my geraniums!" she yelled.

I high-stepped across her garden. "I'm sorry, Miss Dingleberry," I blurted out, messing up her name in my panic. That only made her madder.

"I'm calling your mother, Morgan McCracken!"

I heard a thud behind me.

Dewberry yelled, "I'm calling the cops, Brad Buckholtz!"

Sure enough, Buckholtz hadn't stopped chasing me! I threw a quick look over my shoulder to see how close he was. He'd somehow pulled himself up and over Dewberry's brick wall and fallen face down onto her prized squash plant. Yep, he squashed the squash plant with a face plant.

Buckholtz struggled up and charged after me with yellow squash guts hanging from his hair. He didn't even try to avoid Dewberry's geraniums. In fact, he kicked one of her precious purple plants high into the air. The soil rained down on the old lady's wide-brimmed hat.

I waited for a red traffic light before crossing busy Cypress Avenue while Buckholtz almost caught up. As soon as the light turned green, I raced across the street and zigzagged around lampposts, trashcans, and trees, with Buckholtz closing in behind me. I won't lie to you: I was scared. My heart (which beats over one hundred thousand times a day) was pounding. My lungs were burning. (If your lung tissues were spread out, it would cover a tennis court.) And my legs felt like they were filled with sand. (A sandbag the size of a pillowcase weighs fifty pounds.)

They say that just before you die, events in your entire life—in no particular order—pass before your eyes. I saw a few memorable images as I tore through my neighborhood that day wearing one shoe, with the baby-bird killer in hot pursuit. I saw myself as a lima bean in the kindergarten play; taking the training wheels off my bike; spinning in a Disneyland Mad Hatter teacup; speaking at Grandma Claire's funeral.

I shot down the sidewalk, taking longer and longer strides. But Bradzilla was gaining on me again!

More images ran though my head: catching snowflakes on my tongue; finding out the truth about the Tooth Fairy; chasing fireflies at the Labor Day picnic; snagging a foul ball in my cap at Fenway Park; sleeping in a tent in the backyard all last August.

I hurdled over a low picket fence in front of the house at the end of my block. Buckholtz barely cleared it, stumbled, and then regained his balance.

More pictures of my past: falling off a skateboard and busting my arm; being voted "Most Quiet" in my old school's yearbook; staying up all night holding my dog, Shambles, before he died.

The final vision that flashed across my mind was the moment I first laid eyes on Robin Reynolds, the beautiful girl who lives across the street from our new house.

All in all, it had been a good life—with the exception of the thundering footsteps I heard behind me, growing louder. Brad was within spitting distance, which I knew because he spit on my backpack. (The average human produces ten thousand gallons of saliva in a lifetime, which is enough spit to fill two swimming pools.)

I could see my house at the end of the cul-de-sac. I was exhausted. I didn't think I could outrun Buckholtz any longer.

I was sure that soon he would tackle my legs, drag me to the ground, pin me on my back, dig his knees into my arms—MMA style—and yank each and every red whisker out of my frightened freckled face. And then, of course, he'd murder me.

But suddenly, just as I was about to give up, I heard a mellow voice drift from across the street. It came from Robin Reynolds's perfect lips.

"Hi, Bradley," she said.

Robin had come to collect letters from her mailbox on the curb. She was my age and she sat two aisles away from me in history. She was the most popular girl at school and the prettiest girl in the

Milky Way galaxy. Therefore, we had never spoken. (There are at least one hundred billion galaxies in the universe.)

Buckholtz stopped in his tracks, wheezing, welcoming the interruption, especially by a girl as gorgeous as Robin. I kept running, hobbling with one shoe, my striped boxers hanging out, and my eyes focused on my front door.

I scurried like a scared squirrel down the street in full view of Buckholtz and Robin, scampered into my house, and slammed and locked the door behind me. It was humiliating, especially hearing Buckholtz's hyena laughter. But I was safe. And alive.

I crawled to the window and peeked through the curtains. Buckholtz must have said something stupid because Robin pivoted and stomped back to her house, leaving the big behemoth alone on the sidewalk. He bent over, put his hands on his knees, gasping for air, dripping sweat and squash from his chin onto his stinky vomit-caked boots.

MEET THE MCCRACKENS

I'm a thinker, not a talker. I look at it this way: we have two ears and one mouth. So, we should listen twice as much as we speak. Whatever I do have to say I either keep inside my head, floating in the 80 percent brain water, or I record into my small digital voice recorder (I call it my "McCorder"), which I carry in my pocket at all times. It's my way of jotting down notes and ideas that come to me. Anyway, my sister, Chloe—she's fifteen—does enough talking for both of us.

At dinner, my grandpa saw that I was even more tight-lipped than usual. He always senses when something is bothering me.

Poppy had been living with us since Grandma Claire died. He took Chloe's room, which of course was bigger than mine because she was older and the girl, which meant Chloe moved into my room, which meant I had to move into the basement, which I didn't mind doing because Dad said I could move my workshop from the basement to the attic above the garage, which was much more private, which was better for conducting my secret experiments, which is why I was really happy Poppy moved in with us. That, and because Poppy understood me, maybe better than anyone.

Poppy made me feel okay about being different. He once said, *"Being different means standing out. Standing out means being outstanding."* Everyone should have a grandfather like Poppy.

"I got a 'B' on my Geography test," Chloe boasted as she reached for the salad. Chloe had adjusted quickly and easily to the West Coast and was already popular in our new school. She was a sophomore, an adequate chess player, an aspiring surfer, and the fastest one-thumb texter I'd ever seen. Even though she jabbered nonstop, I guess you could call her cute. Chloe didn't have red hair or freckles like me, because she was adopted.

She piped up again, "I would have gotten a 'B+,' but I got one question wrong—'What is the population of the fifth largest continent?' I mean, really, what sort of lame question is that? Oh, and Stanley Canfield might ask me to the Valentine Day's dance, because Rena Hicks broke up with him at Stephanie Rivera's party, but—"

"There's nothing wrong with a 'B,'" Mom interjected, passing the platter of corn to my dad, who ate in silence. (On average, an ear of corn has eight hundred kernels in sixteen rows.)

"How was *your* day, Morgan?" Mom asked me.

"Okay," I muttered.

My dad stopped chomping on his cob and gave me a long, squinted stare. In our home, dinner is considered the Family News Hour. Chloe and I are expected to talk about our day. One of the rules of giving our nightly report is that we have to be descriptive. Nods, grunts, and one-word answers, like "okay," aren't okay.

"You can do better than that," Mom said.

"Uh, I got plenty of exercise today," I added.

"Exercise?" Mom asked.

"Yeah. I did a lot of running."

Poppy winced, knowing for sure that something shady had happened to me. My dad just shook his head. He needed more details, but luckily Chloe the Chatterbox jumped in.

"You got exercise? Good. Because all you do is sit on your bony butt all day doing your silly research. Such a waste of time."

The vein in Dad's neck began to bulge. He always got upset when Chloe and I teased each other. So he wasn't too pleased when I said to her, "One thousand."

"One thousand what?" Chloe fired back.

"That's the population of the continent of Antarctica, the fifth-largest continent," I said. "Oh, and did you know that if you spell out numbers, you would have to count to one thousand before coming across the letter 'A'? Or that Antarctica is the coldest, windiest, and driest place on earth? I learned all that doing my silly research."

Chloe rolled her eyes.

I responded with, "It takes more than two million working parts in the eye for you to roll them. An ostrich's eye is bigger than its brain. And a worm has no eyes at all." I smiled and added, "Research. Such a silly waste of time."

"Can somebody unplug the McFactoid Machine?" Chloe said.

I had to have the last word. The last factoid. "The continent of Europe has the world's largest country, Russia, and the world's smallest country, Vatican City," I said, taking a little bow. "Ta-dah!" I love being the annoying little brother.

Dad stood up, frowned at Chloe and calmly said, "Go upstairs and clean your room." Then he frowned at me and calmly said, "Clear the table and help Grandpa with the dishes." Then he folded and placed his napkin neatly on the table and calmly said to my mom, "Thanks for dinner, Sweetheart." We all watched in silence as he trudged up the stairs, his feet landing heavily on each step.

Dad had been under a lot of stress lately. He had relocated our family to California because he got a good job as a maintenance engineer at a TV station in San Diego, which is thirty-five minutes away. Poppy moved in to watch Chloe and me while Mom and Dad were at work. Plus, Poppy was tired of the New England winters. But the TV station recently had to lay off a bunch of people, including my dad. A couple nights ago, I overheard him tell Mom that we couldn't live on her bookkeeper's salary alone and if he didn't find work soon, we'd have to sell our new house. It freaked me out. But, I found comfort in remembering that "bookkeeper" is the only word with three consecutive double letters.

Whenever I get flustered or frightened, I concentrate on the random and wacky tidbits collected in my head to calm myself down. Facts are my friends. Facts are always there for me. And that's a fact. In fact, I feel an obscure fact coming on right now: women blink twice as much as men.

I knew that grown-ups were supposed to be the ones to worry about financial problems, but I was worried that we might have to move again, maybe to another city, maybe into a small apartment and that—worst of all—maybe I'd have to share a room with Chloe.

Poppy carried a stack of dirty dishes into the kitchen. I followed with a stack of my own. He and I had our best talks while doing the dishes. He washed and I dried. Dad paid bills upstairs. Chloe gossiped online (instead of cleaning her room) and Mom hummed show tunes while folding laundry. (Did you know that you can't hum if you plug your nose? Go ahead. Try it. I'll wait.)

Poppy was inspecting a dirty fork, when he said, "So, about that 'exercise' you got today . . ."

"I hate him," was all I needed to say.

"Buckholtz again?"

"He's getting faster. What do I do?"

A WISE OLD IRISHMAN

Grandpa and I washed dishes quietly for a few minutes. I didn't say anything. I waited for him to think up a plan for defeating my nemesis: Brad Buckholtz.

Poppy handed me a heavy frying pan to dry.

I raised the pan over my head like a weapon. "If I had this, I wouldn't mind if Brad caught me."

"Nah, you can't fight Buckholtz. He's too tough," Poppy said. "You have to use your strengths." ("Strengths" is the longest word in the English language with just one vowel.)

Poppy had a way of saying things that forced me to think deeper and solve my own problems.

Before he retired, he'd been a barber in Boston for fifty-three years at the same location on Columbus Avenue. He enjoyed listening to other people's troubles and, when asked, giving them advice. He called himself a "cutterologist."

"Seems he picks on you every couple weeks," Poppy said.

"Yeah. He'll be torturing someone else tomorrow. He's an equal opportunity bully."

"Why was he chasing you this time?"

"Because I can grow hair on my face but he can't."

"Bullies. They'll find any excuse to pick a fight."

"If whiskers were like lunch money, I'd give them to him."

Poppy stopped washing the dishes. "I'm sorry he torments you. It's not right."

"I don't know why my whiskers bother him so much."

"I have a theory," Poppy said, scrubbing a pot.

"What?"

"Do you know his father?"

"He's a fisherman. Drinks a lot."

"I bet he's big and tough."

"And has a beard," I said. "His face looks like a tumbleweed with eyeballs."

"Bullies come from bullies, Sparky. It's a hand-me-down trait. Buckholtz wants to prove to himself *and* to his dad that he's a man, but without whiskers he doesn't feel like one."

"And maybe his father makes fun of him for not having any."

"Gotta feel sorry for a kid like that . . . with a father like that."

"Do I have to?"

Poppy put his wet hands on my shoulders. "What *you* have to do is use *your* traits. Use *your* strengths."

"What are my strengths, Poppy?"

"We're McCrackens," he said proudly, tapping the side of his bald head with a soapy finger. "We use our noggins."

I couldn't sleep that night. I had too much going on inside my three-pound brain. (Bullfrogs, ants, and honeybees never sleep. I wondered what they had to worry about. In recent years, honeybee populations across the continent have fallen by as much as 70 percent. That fact alone must keep the bees up at night.)

I gazed at my ceiling, on which I had painted the control panel of the space shuttle in glow-in-the-dark paint.

I turned on my McCorder. "Message to me," I said. "I have to figure out a way to use my noggin to stop Buckholtz from picking on me. I also have to think of an idea that will make money, which will save our house. I also have to get to sleep." (Whales and dolphins only fall *half* asleep. Their brain hemispheres take turns so they can continue surfacing to breathe.)

At five o'clock in the morning, the rattling of old water pipes woke me up. No matter what time it is, whenever someone flushes the toilet or takes a shower in our house, there is loud knocking in the basement pipes. I wondered who was awake so early. I grabbed my emergency, hand-sized, solar-powered light-and-siren combo I invented and tiptoed upstairs to investigate.

Poppy's bathroom door was half open (or was it "half closed?"). He was leaning over the sink, wearing his going-to-church pants. His shirt was off, and he had a towel around his neck. His face was coated with thick, foamy shaving cream. He looked like he had been hit with a cream pie. All you could see were his pale blue eyes. I quietly entered the bathroom and whispered, "Hi, Poppy."

"Top o' the mornin' to ya," he whispered back. "Hope I didn't wake you."

"No. I couldn't sleep," I said. "Where're you going?"

"To a job fair," he said, using a straight-edge razor to even his red sideburns.

"You're looking for a job?"

He stopped shaving and stared at me. "What word is in the word *retired*?" he asked. We always played word games like this.

"Red."

"Longer."

"Tire?"

"Longer."

"Tired?"

"Bingo! I'm *tired*. I'm tired of being *retired*," he said, lifting the tip of his nose to trim the hair on his philtrum. (That's what they call the groove under your nostrils, just above your upper lip.)

I sat on the edge of the bathtub, considering whether to ask my next question. "Is it because we're having money problems?"

Poppy tilted his shiny bald head back, shaving over his Adam's apple. (The Adam's apple is really just an enlarged larynx—your voice box—which becomes big enough to be visible in your neck. While we're on the subject, Adam's apples stick out more in men than women because grown men have larger voice boxes. This is also the reason why dudes speak in deeper tones.) Poppy was careful not to swallow. It was a delicate maneuver, but one he had performed all his adult life on himself and, as a barber, on thousands of others. Poppy is the person who taught me how to shave.

He remained silent. It was clear he didn't want to talk about Mom and Dad's troubles. Through pursed lips he said, "I could've slept another ten minutes if I didn't have to stand here shaving."

"I wish I didn't have to shave either," I said, hating my premature whiskers for making me look different.

"I've spent ten minutes a day for nearly sixty years dragging a blade across my face. That's about—" Poppy tried to do the math.

"Thirty-six hundred hours," I said. "Which is one hundred and fifty days or five months."

Poppy put his razor down on the side of the sink and looked me square in the eyes. "Think about that," he said. "Five months. That's a long time just mowing skin." He wasn't kidding. He was sending me a message.

"There's a wise old Irish saying, Sparky," he whispered. I switched on my McCorder to capture whatever wisdom Poppy was about to impart. He said, "*Time is something you never get back.*"

"Who said that?" I asked him.

"A wise old Irishman." He splashed cold water on his skillfully shaved face. "Now, this McCracken's gotta get crackin,' or he'll be late."

A SOLUTION TO SHAVING

I went back to the basement, got back into bed, and tried to fall back to sleep. (The average person falls to sleep in seven minutes.) But I couldn't keep my mind from working overtime. Poppy's words stayed with me, stirring my imagination and keeping me up. I played them back again on my McCorder: *"Time is something you never get back."* Words worth repeating.

I tossed and turned, then sat up in bed. I needed to distract myself. I turned to one of my inventions: *Morgan's Neighborhood Watch*, a periscope with infrared and camera functions. Dad and I made it out of spare parts we found in a junkyard. We mounted the camera lens on a swing arm fastened to the top of the chimney.

I can lower the eyepiece from my ceiling to my bed by cranking a fishing reel attached to the bed frame. My periscope allows me to keep track of our neighborhood without lifting my head off the pillow.

The contraption slowly descended from the ceiling, stopping in front of my eyes. I set my face inside the eyeshade and wrapped my fingers around the joysticks, moving—by remote control—the lens outside, on top of the roof. I could tilt and pan, swivel 360 degrees, zoom in and zoom out. I could see in the dark. And it all recorded onto a digital memory card, 24/7.

I had an unobstructed view of my neighborhood from high above our cul-de-sac. The streetlamps were just turning off. The automatic sprinklers were just turning on. The newspapers were just being delivered. And the blue jays were landing on the phone lines, squealing their morning song. It was a typical Saturday morning on Crestview Drive, except for one thing: across the street, on the second floor of the Reynolds's home, Robin was resting her elbows on her windowsill, her chin in her hands, her green eyes gazing blankly into the daybreak.

I wondered why she was up before dawn, especially on a Saturday. I wondered what she was thinking about. I wondered if we would ever talk. I wondered if the hottest girl in town and the nerdiest boy in town could ever be friends.

I didn't know much about girls and what made them tick. But I did know this: girls like her weren't interested in boys like me.

I panned my periscope over and saw my seventy-three-year-old grandfather, all dressed up, wearing his Boston Red Sox cap on his bald head, shuffling down the street to the bus stop.

I cranked the fishing reel and the eyepiece rose, returning to my ceiling. I finally gave up on the idea of sleep and climbed out of bed. And shaved.

I needed some fresh air. I went outside to our small backyard. My pet tortoise, Taxi, who wasn't allowed in the house, was nibbling his breakfast in our garden, where Poppy grew lettuce for him.

Taxi was the size of a dinner plate. The thick skin on his front legs looked like the bark of a tree, and his hind legs looked like they had plates of armor attached. His shell resembled a rusty old army helmet. And he had the face of E. T. I loved him.

I picked Taxi up and sat on the patio swing. He liked rocking in my lap. Although Taxi didn't do tricks like the late-great Shambles or cuddle like our calico cat, Kitten Kaboodle, he was a loyal companion and would last longer than any other kind of pet. In fact, tortoises can live up to 150 years.

I liked talking to Taxi. When I heard my own voice, it helped me get my thoughts straight. "Maybe," I said to him, "I could come up with something that would save people the time it takes to shave. Maybe I could design a faster razor. Maybe I could create a superior shaving cream."

I lifted Taxi high, like an offering to the Gods. "Maybe, just maybe, I could invent something that would stop whiskers from growing and eliminate the need to shave altogether!"

I stood up with Taxi in my arms. "If I could find a solution to shaving, I'd never have to go to school again with stubble on my face. I'd never be teased again. If I could develop a product that everybody in the world would buy and use every day, I'd be rich and famous. Then Dad and Poppy wouldn't have to find jobs, Mom could quit hers, we could keep our house, I could keep my basement bedroom, Buckholtz and the other kids at school would think I was cool, and maybe even Robin would look past my red hair and freckles and say 'hi' to me."

Taxi blinked one eye at a time, and then his head retreated into his shell. (The muscle that lets the human eye blink is the fastest muscle in your body. It allows you to blink five times a second. I bet you're trying it right now.)

I continued to think aloud, "I've gotta get McCrackin' on my new invention, Taxi, because *time is something you can never get back*."

I marched with purpose across the backyard, lifted the garage door, and went inside. We used the garage for storage, leaving our cars parked in the driveway. Leading up to the attic was a trapdoor in the ceiling. I opened the combination lock (08-29-58: the birthday of my favorite singer, Michael Jackson) on the attic door latch and pulled the rope handle attached to the trapdoor. I unfolded the narrow wooden stepladder. With Taxi firmly in hand, I climbed the ten steps up to my laboratory loft.

As I entered my lab (I call it the *McFactory*), I said loudly and proudly, "Yeah, I'm a McCracken!" Taxi's head poked out from under his shell to hear more. "My strength is my brain. And my brain can solve all my problems!"

A husky voice cried out. "Quiet!"

THE MCFACTORY

I switched on the light in the garage attic. Staring at me from across the room were the black gleaming eyes of Echo, my parrot . . . my Red-lored Amazon, as they are known. She was in her cage, which hung over my lab table.

"Sorry, ma'am. I didn't mean to disturb you," I whispered.

"Nighty night!" she said, closing her eyes and falling back to sleep.

Most Red-lored Amazons enjoy the company of humans. Not Echo. They told us at the Parrot Rescue Center that Echo was a loner (like me) and preferred to hang out in a cage filled with lots of toys and plenty of seeds, fruits, and vegetables. Echo may not have been social, but she was one brainy bird. She had a vocabulary of a thousand words, a photographic memory, and one cocky attitude. Lately, she had been showing an interest in the outside world, perching on the windowsill and bird watching by the hour. The Rescue Center said that someday she might want to be released into the wild where she would join one of many parrot colonies in Carlsbad.

The *McFactory* had a large front window and a large side window, running water, electricity, and heat. It was like having the world's greatest tree house, and I spent as much time as I could in it.

My parents let me decorate the space any way I wanted. So I had painted a map of the world on the floor and the periodic table on the ceiling, and I pasted posters of famous redheads on the walls: Conan O'Brien, Lucille Ball, Little Orphan Annie, Thomas Jefferson, Bozo the Clown, Ed Sheeran, and Shaun White. I also put up posters of some of my favorite inventors: Thomas Edison (holds 1,093 US patents!), Alexander Graham Bell (telephone), Levi Strauss (jeans), Kane Kramer (iPod), Jack Dorsey (Twitter), and Louis Reard (bikini). I'm particularly thankful to Mr. Reard.

In one corner of the room was my dad's old reading lamp and a perfectly good recliner that I found in the alley. In that chair, I did my best thinking and my best napping.

In the opposite corner was a large secondhand blackboard on wheels that I used to organize my thoughts, work out problems, and write down computations.

In the center of the room was my lab table—our old kitchen door set on a couple of two-drawer metal file cabinets. On the table were papers, beakers, Bunsen burners, glass tubing, funnels, bell jars, Petri dishes, vials, chemicals, magnets, minerals, test tubes, balance scales, and other junk. I swept some stuff aside and set Taxi on the table.

On the far side of the room was a workshop area complete with a sawhorse, a workbench, a used band saw, a refurbished drill press, and a tool rack I made out of pegboard.

Along the walls, I had shelves stacked with reference books, a mini-refrigerator, potted plants, an antique cast iron safe, a rusty supply cabinet, a well-worn steamer trunk, and two fire extinguishers. I had an old coffee table and a broken-down couch that converted into a sofa bed to sleep in on nights when the basement got too hot or too cold or too noisy.

I received a wireless Internet signal from the modem in our house, so I was connected to the web day and night.

To keep me company, I had a snake named Nixon, a mouse called Mickey, and a rat known as Madoff. And of course there was Echo, my arrogant, colorful, and brilliant bird. She enjoyed a spacious redwood cage that my dad built with me. It was large enough for five parrots.

I picked up a pitcher from the table and quietly filled Echo's water bowl. I think she was grateful that I never clipped her wings. I let her fly around the *McFactory* for exercise whenever she wanted.

I loved the *McFactory*. It was here that I allowed my mind to wander . . . and wonder. It was here that I hatched many of my ideas.

It was here that I built *Morgan's Firewall* (also known as *Don't Even Think About It!*), an alarm system that detected motion outside my bedroom door and set off a screeching noise and a flashing red light when intruders came near. (The color red doesn't really make bulls angry. Bulls are colorblind. It's the movement of the cape, not the color, that excites them.)

"Naturally, red is my favorite color," I said to Taxi, scooping him up off the table. "While we're at it, 27 is my favorite number, because if you add up all the numbers between 2 and 7, the total is 27. And 27 reminds me of my favorite planet: Uranus, which has 27 known moons." The image of Uranus and mooning made me laugh my butt off, which unfortunately woke Echo. She squawked and flapped her wings.

"Sorry, again, Echo." I carried Taxi over to my supply cabinet. "But we're not here to think about planets or moons. We're here to invent the solution to shaving. Do you see anything in here that can help?"

I had plenty of spare parts to use. My dad had kept all of the used equipment from the TV studio. He always brought home left-over supplies and old, thrown-out parts from the station. Instead of stacking blocks when I was a baby, I stacked spools of speaker cable. Instead of playing with toy trains, I played with broken down transistors, transformers, and transponders.

"I need a device of some sort," I said aloud, scanning the supply cabinet inventory. "Can I run a laser or invisible sound waves over my skin to make the whiskers stop growing?"

I rubbed my freshly shaved chin, thinking. Maybe it would be better to go with some kind of lotion, some kind of ointment that sealed the skin.

I placed Taxi on the painted floor map, just over the continent of Africa, from where his ancestors originally came. (Message to me: "Tell Chloe that Africa is the *second* largest and the *most* popu-lated continent in the world.") Above Africa, on my ceiling periodic table was Zn (Zinc, element #30). (Since 1982, US-minted "cop-per" pennies have actually been 97.6 percent zinc, with just a 2.4 percent copper coating. Hey, you never know when someone will ask you about that.)

But enough stalling. It was time to start inventing. I loved the challenge of trying to think of something that never existed before. Something altogether new. Something that would solve a problem that's been around since the first whisker sprouted on the first face.

Something that could change people's lives forever. I sank deeply into my recliner chair to do some deep thinking.

Every great inventor knows that great successes come from many small failures and that lesser inventions come before greater ones. I set my mind on *reverse* mode, thinking back to see if any of my past inventions could aid me with my current project.

Over the years, I had rigged my basement bedroom with gizmos and gadgets. I had built the *Neighborhood Watch Camera* on the roof, my *Automatic Bed Maker*, and my *Mastermind 5000*—a voice-controlled activator that followed simple verbal commands like, "lights on," or "iPod off," or "MP3 player on," and so on. (To give verbal commands, we rely on vibrating vocal chords, which are only the size of our thumbnails.)

I'd also had my share of unsuccessful inventions. But as Thomas Edison said, "Just because something doesn't do what you planned it to do, doesn't mean it's useless." So I thought over my, uh, less-than-successful inventions as well, in case they offered lessons that would help me now.

I thought about my inflatable dartboard. That one had let the air out of my inventing career for a while.

I'd also invented *Fan-tastic Paint*. If you tie an open paint can to a ceiling fan, you can very quickly spread paint on your walls. Warning: your room will look like Jackson Pollock (look him up) barfed all over.

My drinkable shampoo, which I called *SodaPoo* (a really bad name), was a big bust as well.

"But I can't fail this time, Taxi," I said. "I need to come up with an anti-beard growth formula so that Brad will leave me alone and men everywhere will have more time."

"More time, more time!" Echo dittoed.

"Here's the assignment." I popped up from my chair, paced across the room, over Tunisia and under Tellurium, and I wrote the words *Hair Today, Gone Tomorrow* on the blackboard.

"Imagine no more razors, shaving cream, razor blades, or after-shave lotions. Imagine no more going to school with little pieces of toilet paper stuck to your face covering nicks." I paused for a moment. "Imagine nobody making fun of your stubble ever again. Just imagine."

"Just imagine," Echo echoed.

I sat back down in my recliner, closed my eyes, and began to imagine, pondering the possibilities of a beard-free world. In order to stop whiskers from growing, I needed to understand how they *started* growing. By knowing all the facts, by applying some mighty McCracken mind power, by making some lucky guesses, I could save three billion men in the world ten minutes of their lives each day! Ten minutes they would never get back.

"Just imagine!" Echo said again, before falling back to sleep.

(The song "Imagine" by John Lennon of The Beatles was the best-selling single of his solo career.)

THE MYSTIFYING FEMALE SPECIES

The next thing I remember, Mom was shouting from outside, "Morgan! Now!"

I had fallen deep asleep in my deep thinking chair. It was already noon. And I hadn't done my Saturday morning chores. The punishment for not doing my Saturday chores was no lab privileges on Sunday. I couldn't let that happen. I was on a mission.

In order to exit the *McFactory* fast, I executed my "emergency jump," an athletic leap from the opening of the hatch to the garage floor, vaulting over all the trapdoor stairs. I landed hard onto the cement floor, grabbed the broom out of the garage, and hurried to the front yard.

I was sweeping the leaves off the sidewalk in front of my house, thinking of different components I could mix together for my formula, when I heard someone call out, "Hi." It was the goddess from across the street. I almost lost my balance.

Was she talking to *me*? Couldn't be. But what if she were? I had to be sure. I looked behind me, confirming that I was the only one around. I pointed to my chest and cocked my head like a puppy. She nodded and took a step in my direction. Was this really happening?

"Hi," I said, excited to have exchanged our first words (all four letters).

"Buckholtz is such a baby, isn't he?" Robin said, walking leisurely toward me.

I raised the broom above my head, indicating Buckholtz's height, and said, "Yeah, but a *big* baby."

Robin remained focused, continuing to cross the street, like in slow motion. Her black ponytail bounced softly. I noticed that her emerald green eyes were red from lack of sleep or from crying.

"Where did you learn to run so fast?" she asked.

"At my old school."

"Were you on the track team?"

"No. I seem to attract bullies."

"I'm Robin," she said, joining me on the sidewalk.

"I know," I said. "I'm Morgan."

"I know," she said.

My heart beat hard as we shook hands, her hand in mine. She knew my name? "I live over there," she said, pointing to her two-story house.

"I know. I live over here," I said.

"I know," she said.

"I guess we know a lot about each other." Spoken like a true geeknoid. I shifted from one foot to the other. Neither of us said anything else. We just stood there. Some guys always know exactly what to say to girls. They can keep the conversation going, making girls laugh, making them feel like one of the guys, but more special. They know how to get girls to like them. Where did they learn how to do that? Why didn't anyone teach me? How much longer would Robin stay there without my speaking? I really didn't want her to leave. She was watching a seagull circle overhead, waiting for me to say something, *anything*. So was I.

It takes the interaction of seventy-two muscles to produce human speech. I finally managed to force enough of my mouth muscles to utter something.

"I like your ponytail."

"It's just hair," she fired back.

I was so flustered I didn't know what to say next. My noggin took over. I went to my auto-response, my default, my fail-safe trivia. "So Robin, did you know that the robin is the official state bird of Connecticut, Michigan, and—"

"Wisconsin," Robin said.

"Right," I said. "And did you know that 'Q' is the only letter in the alphabet that doesn't appear in the name of any of the states in America?"

"That's because 'Q' is the least-used letter in the English language," she said. "And did you know there's a tiny town in Nebraska named *Morgan*?"

This was getting interesting. Robin knew strange and little-known stuff like I did. Stuff like Morgan, Nebraska (population 132, incidentally).

I was still mostly surprised that she knew my name. I wondered if she wanted to know more about me. Could we actually be friends? Could we be *more* than friends? The answer came quickly.

"Well, gotta go," she said. She started to walk across the street back to her house.

I knew it was too good to be true. She was just trying to be neighborly. Robin Reynolds certainly didn't need any more friends. She wasn't going to waste time talking to someone who couldn't talk. I dropped my head and resumed sweeping the walkway until Robin turned and called out, "Why was he chasing you?"

I looked up with renewed hope. "He's jealous that I shave," I called back.

"Then, I guess he's jealous of me, too."

"You shave?"

"Half the girls at school shave, dummy. It's no big deal."

I couldn't believe I was speaking to Robin Reynolds, especially about shaving. I didn't want it to end, even if she did call me "dummy."

"What if you didn't have to shave?" I asked.

"My legs would look like a woolly mammoth's."

I laughed. She didn't.

"I mean, what if someone invented something so you'd never have to shave again?" I asked.

She thought for a moment and hollered back, "If someone hasn't invented it by now, no one ever will."

Just as I was about to thank her for stopping Buckholtz from catching and killing me, she said, "See ya."

I watched her step onto her front porch and open the door. She stopped, spun around, and said, "There are more stars in space than there are grains of sand on every beach on Earth, in case you were wondering."

"Every star you see in the night sky is bigger and brighter than the sun," I said in return. "In case you were wondering." That fact didn't seem to impress her. She just stared at the "dummy" and went inside her house.

I stood there feeling feelings I had never felt before. I felt that I might have made my first Carlsbad friend. I felt a real connection between Robin and me. Suddenly, the front door to her house flung open. Robin stood there in the doorway with her hand on her hip and yelled, "I'm more than my ponytail, you know!" She slammed the door hard.

I shook my head, leaned on my broom and tried to figure out what she meant. Had I said something wrong? Was this what girls were like? Would we ever talk again? Did I blow it? As I contemplated why our first chat ended so badly, her front door flew open once more, her head popped out and she shouted, "Hair can't be stopped from growing! It's impossible!" Again, she slammed her door. Harder than the first time.

Maybe girls spoke in riddles. Maybe she was challenging me. I knew a lot about a lot of things, but I knew nothing about the female species. Parrots were easier to understand. Turtles were a snap. But girls were well beyond my comprehension.

I knew this, though: Robin was as smart as she was beautiful. And up close, she looked like a movie star.

More than ever, I felt motivated to continue my shave-no-more quest. I'd show the world that I could do the impossible, that I could invent something nobody had invented yet. I'd prove that I was more than red stubble and freckles. I'd show Robin Reynolds that Morgan McCracken was a dummy she would want to be friends with. Or *more* than friends with.

Poppy came walking up the street. His necktie was loosened, his coat was draped over his arm, and he was smiling.

"Did you get a job?" I asked.

"Nope."

"What did they say?"

"Let me think. Oh, yeah . . . *'you're too damn old.'*"

Then he laughed. "No problem," he said. "It's like fishing. I'll get one next time."

Poppy was an optimist. Nothing ever seemed to get him down. Nothing was impossible for my grandpa. Nothing should be impossible for his grandson.

MORGAN FOR PRESIDENT

Unluckily for him but luckily for me, Buckholtz contracted mononucleosis and was out for the rest of the semester. I wondered who would ever kiss him. Isn't that how you catch that disease? Come to think of it, I wish I had caught mononucleosis . . . from Robin Reynolds. Here's a fact I wished I *didn't* know: Morgan McCracken had never kissed a girl. And a girl had never kissed him. I guess that's the same pathetic thing.

I could barely talk with a girl. How could I ever kiss one? Of course, you don't have to talk while you're kissing. I actually had taken an acting class last summer hoping to be assigned a love scene where I had to kiss a girl. Instead, I was given a Shakespearean monologue that took all of July to memorize.

My first kiss would be a long, long way off.

As an inquisitive kind of fact-gathering guy, I have done quite a bit of research on the subject of kissing. Things I learned: Lips are more sensitive than the tips of the fingers. Two-thirds of people turn their heads to the right when kissing. The X's at the end of a correspondence are meant to be what two faces look like during a kiss.

Morgan McFactoid at your lip-locking service!

Anyway, with Buckholtz down with mono and with Robin seemingly mad at me for mysterious reasons unknowable to me, I could concentrate on my search for a solution to shaving. I went to the library and read everything on the subject of facial hair, which wasn't much. I stayed up late Googling "hair follicles," "beard growth," and "whiskers." I found out that:

- The average man's face contains up to fifteen thousand whiskers. (I counted over three hundred red ones on my face. More red whiskers than red freckles.)
- Men's beards grow at a rate of about half an inch per month (six inches per year).
- A man will shave at least twenty thousand times in his lifetime.
- Archeologists believe that cavemen used clams and shark teeth to shave with twenty thousand years ago in the Stone Age. Ouch!
- The longest beard ever recorded was on Hans Langseth of Norway. It stretched seventeen feet and six inches. (That's way longer than Dad's Jeep!)
- A man removes over twenty-seven feet of hair in his lifetime through shaving. (Ah, twenty-seven, my favorite number again. Twenty-seven is also the number of bones in the human hand.)

💡 And here's one for Robin: women have been pulling, pluck-
ing, burning, tweezing and ripping out their leg and armpit
hair as far back as 4000 BC, when they were using dangerous
substances like arsenic and quicklime to get the job done.

Before I spent any more time on my idea, before I went any further
with my plans, I needed to know if I was on the right track, if my
shave-no-more project was really worth pursuing. I wanted to get
some professional feedback. ("Feedback" is the shortest word that
contains the letters A, B, C, D, E, and F.)

While drying the dinner dishes, I talked to a true hair expert,
the former barber, the cutterologist. He would give me his wisdom
and honest opinion.

"Poppy, I've been working on a new invention. It's a secret."

"If it's a secret, then you better not tell me," he said.

"It's an idea that would save you lots of time."

"They already invented the dishwasher."

We both laughed. Then, I said in low tones, "I'm going to invent
something that will save time, money, and energy. Something that
men and women everywhere will use, every day. Something that
stops body hair from growing."

"I'm afraid, Sparky, that hair grows like weeds, for which bar-
bers are most grateful."

"But—"

"Besides, we need hair. The hair on your head, arms, and legs keeps
you warm and dry. Eyelashes keep dirt and sweat from getting in your
eyes. The thick hair in your nostrils acts like a filter, keeping you healthy."

"But—"

"Bones. Fingernails. Hair. We need them all and they all grow.
You can't stop Mother Nature from doing her job." He handed me
a saucepan to dry.

"But, if I could save you from shaving, then you could get some extra sleep every morning," I said.

Poppy thought about that for a moment, then said, "There's a wise, old Irish saying . . ." I turned on the McCorder. *"No dreamer is too small; no dream too big,"* he said. "You've always been a dreamer. Don't let anybody, including me, discourage any of your ideas—your dreams—no matter how far-fetched or harebrained they seem to be." He returned to washing the dishes and said, "Who knows, you could be a whisker away from a great discovery."

Exactly the feedback I was looking for.

I worked days and nights trying to develop the exact blend of ingredients to prevent beard growth. I used all my scientific research and personal instincts, testing one mixture after another, experimenting on myself. I tried combination after combination, changing the measurements of each element. I documented each test in my McCorder, listing aloud the different components. I tried bicycle grease, tile caulk, candle wax—anything I could think of that would block beard hair from sprouting. I put some of Mom's bath oil in, as well, so that my formula would smell good.

I smeared each lotion on my face every night before going to bed, the theory being that the gooey solution would stop hair from poking up through the skin and by the time I awoke the next morning, I would appear cleanly shaven.

My product would be known as *WhiskAway,* an anti-shaving cream that took effect while you slept. Apply in seconds at night, and by morning you can skip shaving and stay in bed a little longer. Who wouldn't want that?

But I experienced failure after failure. One morning, I woke up with a green rash all over my face. (That was fun to go to school with.) Another morning, I woke up with a blue rash all over my face. (Another humiliating day at school.) And every morning, red stubble still covered my skin, ready to be sheared. I was losing faith. Maybe Robin was right. If Einstein couldn't figure this one out, how could I? (In 1952, Albert Einstein was offered the presidency of Israel. He turned it down.)

I was determined, though. One way or the other, I was going to whip the shaving problem. If I stopped facial hair from growing, maybe some country would offer to make *me* its clean-shaven head of state. I'd accept.

President Morgan McCracken. I liked the sound of that.

But as the days went on, I ran out of ideas. Nothing was working. I had tried every compound and every combination I could think of. I was stumped. I didn't know what else to do, other than give in . . . give up . . . admit defeat.

But Poppy always says, *"A winner is someone who gets up one more time than he is knocked down."*

I promised myself I'd get up one more time. After all, the presidency was at stake.

A PINCH OF THIS, A DASH OF THAT

On a cold Monday night, dark clouds moved in. I could hear the wind chimes clanging and light rain pelting the garage roof. I had brought Taxi inside the *McFactory*, out of the approaching storm. I sat on my lab stool in front of a mirror, holding a large magnifying glass, studying my facial hair, and hoping it was the last time I'd ever see it. (Hair on your face and head grows faster than hair on the rest of your body.)

Having exhausted every idea and seeing every prior experiment fail, on that night I decided to give *WhiskAway* one last chance, one final test. If it proved successful, I would awake with a smooth face and on the brink of becoming a very important twenty-first century inventor. If I were unsuccessful, I would continue to be known as the freckled-face kid with the red whiskers, doomed to suffer more teasing and taunting.

"Taxi," I said to my tortoise, "tonight's the night we're going to McCracken the problem."

Taxi took a baby step toward me, which I interpreted as a sign of support.

"There is a time in every inventor's life when a miracle *must* happen. My time is now!"

"Miracle!" Echo screeched. "Now!"

There was a flash of lightning, followed by the sound of rolling thunder. The lamps in the lab flickered.

"*Squwaaack!*" Echo squealed and flapped her wings.

"Don't be scared, Echo. It's just a storm. You're safe in here."

I studied the chalk notes on my blackboard, reviewing the latest and last version of my secret formula. I lined up all the containers of all my ingredients; each was a common household item. I'll be honest: at this point I didn't really know what I was doing or what to expect. I confess—this last shot would be more about guesswork and luck than science and skill.

As I was about to speak into the McCorder to name each substance and describe each portion, I realized the batteries were dead. I plugged the McCorder in, but I wasn't about to wait for it to recharge.

"Remind me, Echo, to always keep my batteries charged," I said.

"Always keep my batteries charged," Echo said.

"Thank you," I said.

"Thank you," she said.

Echo stuck her little head out of one of the holes in the bottom of her cage. She liked watching me work on the lab table below her.

I picked up my first item, turned to my gallery of pets and said, "Okay, guys. This is it. We start with a smidgen of rubber cement."

As I mentioned each element, one by one, I dropped them into a steel blender on my lab table:

- a dash of mud (A "dash" is equal to an eighth of a teaspoon.)
- a dab of comb honey (Honeybees beat their wings 11,400 times per minute. The beating of their wings is what makes the buzzing noise.)
- a pinch of salt (Put a few grains of rice in your salt shaker for easier pouring.)
- a broccoli stem (I hate broccoli.)
- a squirt of maple syrup (I love syrup.)
- a quarter-tube of toothpaste (How *do* they get toothpaste in the tube? Well, I'm glad you asked. They shoot the tube with paste from the bottom, and then seal the end. The cap is already in place when the tube is filled.)
- a half-cup of buttermilk (Which has no butter in it. Did you know that?)
- a squeeze of kumquat (They are like reverse oranges: the peel is sweet, and the pulp inside is sour.)
- three egg yolks (The average hen lays over 250 eggs a year!)
- four kidney beans (Kidney beans are named that because they are shaped like a human kidney.)
- a two-dollar bill (Hey, why not?)
- an aspirin (Adding aspirin to water in a vase will make cut flowers last longer.)
- three garlic cloves (The smell of garlic can be removed by running your hands under cold water while rubbing a stain-less steel object.)

- 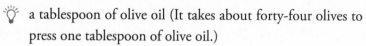 a tablespoon of olive oil (It takes about forty-four olives to press one tablespoon of olive oil.)
- a drizzle of chocolate sauce (I couldn't help eating some.)
- a clump of grass (I didn't eat any. But Taxi did.)
- three marshmallows (Americans buy 90 million pounds of marshmallows each year, about the same weight as 1,286 gray whales.)
- a teaspoon of mouthwash (You can use mouthwash to clean and disinfect germs in your toilet bowl. Better yet, have your sister do it!)
- a small can of tuna (Now you know why the mouthwash.)
- a scoop of bacon bits (A 250-pound pig yields twenty-three pounds of bacon.)
- two peanuts (Peanuts are one of the ingredients in dynamite. Gee, what if I blew up my lab?)
- a thimble full of Tabasco sauce (I put Tabasco sauce on *everything.* So why not on my face?)
- a cap full of baby powder (I love the smell. It reminds me of my youth.)
- a slice of candied apple (I ate the rest.)
- one walnut (Walnuts are the oldest known tree food—they date back to 10,000 BC!)
- a half-pack of Milk Duds (I ate the other half. Do you see a sugar theme developing here?)
- a banana peel (You can use the inside of a banana peel to clean and polish leather shoes.)
- a stick of cinnamon (Cinnamon was used in ancient Egypt for the process of mummification and as an ingredient of perfumes.)

"And that's it," I said.

"And that's it," Echo said.

With all my ingredients inside Mom's old blender, I turned it to the "puree" setting for thirty-three seconds—not thirty-two, not thirty-four, but exactly thirty-three seconds—mixing the solution all together. (Thirty-three, because the longest professional baseball game in history went thirty-three innings.)

Now I was ready to try my experiment. With two fingers I scooped some of my concoction out of the blender. It smelled like double mint gum. The pudding-like substance was warm, sticky, and deep purple. (No word in the English language rhymes with "purple" or "silver." Or "month," for that matter.) There, in my hand, was my final attempt for *WhiskAway*.

I slathered and sealed my face with the purple gunk, then turned to my pets and announced, "Shaving robs us of time—time that we can never get back. Unwanted facial hair is a time killer. So it's time for unwanted facial hair to be destroyed! Down with beards!"

"Aye, aye, Matey!" Echo said. That was her favorite expression. I think she wanted to be a pirate's parrot.

Again, lightning lit up the lab. Again, a clap of thunder rattled the windows, and Echo's nerves.

"Aye, aye, aye, aye, AYE!" Echo screamed. "Scared!"

"Calm down, Echo. Don't poop your feathers. It's just thunder," I said.

For safekeeping, I placed my laptop computer inside the waterproof backpack I had invented and prepared to leave the *McFactory*. Even though Taxi had his protective shell (*his* waterproof backpack!), I decided to let him stay inside the attic that night. I didn't want him to be out in the rain. He would be warm and dry in the lab. And I was sure my petrified parrot could use his company.

I climbed down the attic steps, locked the trapdoor behind me, and sprinted through the driving rain across the backyard to the house, into my cozy underground bedroom. ("Underground" is the only word that begins and ends with "und.")

Wind whistled through the trees as the rainstorm pounded the roof. (Every minute, 907 tons of precipitation falls on earth.) I changed into my pajamas and crawled into bed, eager to feel my face the next morning. I thought the teeth-rattling bursts of thunder would keep me up all night, but I soon fell into a deep sleep.

I dreamt of hair that night. ("Dreamt" is the only English word that ends in the letters "mt.") I dreamt that I never cut my red locks or shaved my red beard. I looked like a Neanderthal in striped boxers. There were large, purple insects living in my hair . . . I tripped over my beard and my head became too heavy with facial hair to hold itself upright . . . I was forced to walk stooped over. I dragged my knuckles along the ground . . . I grunted like an ape . . . the National Guard captured me with a net. They put me on display in the zoo . . . small children pointed and laughed at me . . . old lady Dewberry threw snakes, mice, and rats at me . . . Buckholtz spit Tabasco sauce on me. I caught mononucleosis ... Bozo the Clown called me "Hairy". . . the newspaper called me a freak . . . and my own parrot called me a dummy.

The nightmare ended when a pretty princess named Robin opened my wooden cage and helped me escape inside a giant marshmallow . . . which floated to Antarctica. Lady Robin waited every night in her bedroom . . . looking out her upstairs window . . . hoping that someday the Duke of Morgan would return . . . as president . . . and kiss her.

A FLOOD, A FLOP, AND A
FIRST-CLASS FIASCO

An earsplitting crack of thunder startled me awake as the rare Southern California thunderstorm raged outside my basement window. I sat straight up in bed. My alarm clock read 1:00 a.m. I quickly grabbed my flashlight and a hand mirror next to my bed and examined my face.

The purple chemical mask was plastered firmly in place with no signs of any beard growth. I knew it was still early, but I was feeling confident that a cosmetic first was in the making and that, in just a few more hours, I would awake to a whiskerless face. Very soon, fame and fortune would be mine!

I was so excited I couldn't fall back to sleep, so I decided to distract myself by seeing how the neighborhood was holding up in the monster storm. I lowered my periscope. I looked in the eyeshade and out at our cul-de-sac. A torrential rain continued to pour, and a wild wind whipped the telephone wires. I noticed that the streetlights flickered on and off, as did all the houselights on the block. I deduced that the storm was repeatedly knocking out electricity in our area. I saw a candle flame shimmering through the drapes in Robin's room.

"I wonder if she's awake," I said to myself. "I wonder if she's afraid of the storm. I wonder if she's thinking of our conversation. Or if she ever thinks of me."

I turned the periscope lens on the roof around 180 degrees to look through the large window of my lab above the garage. I could see Echo's cage swaying in the wind. Taxi was sleeping peacefully on the floor. He had crawled under my lab stool, which was under Pt (platinum, element #78) and on top of Sweden. (Swedes have the longest life expectancy of all Europeans.)

I reeled the periscope back to the ceiling. The storm was growing even stronger and the wind howling even louder. In order to safeguard our belongings in the garage, I was going to get out of my warm and cozy bed, run outside, and close the garage door. But I lay there too long thinking about it and fell back to sleep.

I awoke abruptly the next morning. I could see through my basement window that it was a bright, sunny California day again without a cloud in the sky. I rubbed my eyes and excitedly fumbled around for the hand mirror.

The time had come. This was the critical morning-after stubble check. In the very next instant, I would either be a celebrity inventor or a kid in need of a shave.

I took a deep breath, opened my eyes, hoped for a miracle, and looked at my reflection in the mirror. The result? I was a kid in need of a shave.

To my great disappointment, red stubble had grown overnight on my purple face and was waiting patiently to be cut.

WhiskAway was a failure. A flop. A first-class fiasco.

So much for changing my life with one fantastic formula, one incredible discovery. So much for being rich and famous. So much for becoming president. I buried my head in the pillows and just rested there until the motion detector alarm went off, indicating someone had approached my door, breaching the perimeter. I checked the small TV monitor on my bedside table and saw Dad staring into the surveillance camera, which I had embedded on the outside of my door. I said, "Admit," and the voice-activated *Mastermind 5000* automatically unlocked and swung open my bedroom door.

"Get dressed. We have some work to do," Dad said, stepping into my room.

"What kind of work?"

"Cleaning up. Last night's storm made a real mess." He moved closer. "What's that on your face?"

"Uh, uh, pimple cream. Purple pimple paste."

"Oh. Anyway, I've been straightening up the garage. Seems someone left the door open. Haven't had a chance to check out your lab, but—"

I immediately forgot about my beard-growth defeat as all thoughts went to my pets. Still in my pajamas, I slipped on my flip-flops, scooted passed my father, and ran up the basement stairs, out of the house, and through the puddles in the backyard. Mud splattered all over me.

On the ground in the backyard, I saw evidence of the storm's damage: shingles from the roof, bricks from the chimney, and downed branches from our elm tree. The concrete birdbath had toppled over and crushed Taxi's cage. I was grateful that I had left him safe inside the lab. That is, I *hoped* he was safe.

I raced into the garage. All the stuff inside was soaked and strewn about. On my way to the attic door, I had to step over old paint cans, trophies, skis, suitcases, bikes, tennis racquets, rakes, canned goods, Dad's fishing poles, Mom's bookkeeping files, Chloe's teddy bear collection, boxes of worn clothing, photo albums, and gardening equipment. Everything was a mess. I would have to "Morganize" it all later.

"I'm coming, guys!" I yelled to the animals. Then, I saw something that made my eyes pop. There was water gushing out the sides of the trapdoor onto the garage floor. I opened the combination lock to the door and pulled on the rope handle. The door was jammed!

I snatched our extension ladder, lugged it to the side of the garage, and leaned it against the wall, under the side window. I scrambled up. The window glass was completely shattered. Probably by a branch or some flying object. Being careful not to cut myself on shards of glass still clinging to the window frame, I stepped off the ladder into the attic. My mouth fell open as I took in the sight.

The *McFactory* was in ruins. All my posters were ripped to shreds. Light bulbs had blown out. Everything that had been on shelves had come down. Everything that had been stored in cabinets had come out. My furniture was tossed over, and on my lab table, beakers had been knocked over and broken. My reference books were floating among other debris in four inches of water. My blackboard was washed clean of all my computations. Fortunately, my waterproof backpack had protected my laptop from any water damage. More fortunately, the cages of Nixon the snake, Mickey the mouse, and Madoff the rat were high enough off the floor so that none of them had drowned.

And though the lid had blown off my heavy steel blender, the mighty mixer was still upright, its contents still inside.

Echo was shaking, but safe in her cage, suspended high above the flooded floor. But my little tortoise was nowhere to be seen. I searched through the rubble for Taxi.

"Taxi!" I called out.

"Taxi!" Echo screamed.

Then, in the far corner of the room, just above a submerged New Zealand, just below He (Helium, element #2), I spotted Taxi. He had somehow made his way onto a seat cushion, which had served as a flotation device, and he had drifted to safety. I waded over and scooped him up. His shell was filthy and smelled like a dirty sock.

"You must've had a heck of a night, Taxi."

He tucked his head back into his shell. I could tell he was pretty tired. And shell-shocked.

"Heck of a night, heck of a night!" Echo chimed in.

I took the back of my sleeve and started to clean the excess mud off of Taxi's back. As I was scrubbing him, I began to think that maybe I wouldn't rebuild my lab, that maybe I should stop doing crazy experiments and take up a new hobby, like 3D photography or ghost hunting or kite surfing. Maybe I should give up trying to impress everybody—or one somebody—by inventing the impossible.

As I was finishing my last thought, Chloe called out from the backyard below, "Morgan, are you up there?" She always sounded irked.

"No," I called back, to irk her some more.

"Mom wants me to help you clean the attic," she yelled. "But since you never *ever* let anyone in your precious lab, I'm sure you're going to say you don't need my help."

"For once, you're right," I yelled back.

"Good," she said. "That's not all."

"What else?" I called out.

"I'm tired of shouting. Come to the window."

I set Taxi on my footstool, sloshed my way through the flood-water and broken glass to the side window, and looked out. Chloe was standing with Robin.

"You have a visitor," Chloe said.

A FUZZ-FINDING FRIEND

I stared down, nervous, but pleased that Robin had come to my house, had come to see me, and that maybe, just maybe, we were about to speak again.

She looked up. "I left my history book in the backseat of my mom's car. And she left the window down. And because of last night's rain, my history book is now . . . well, history."

"Nice pj's, Morgan," Chloe said, never missing a chance to humiliate me.

"Could I borrow yours for a couple hours?" Robin asked.

"My pj's?" I asked.

"Your history book, Jerkus!" Chloe said.

Robin knew lots of people who she could have borrowed the history book from. Why did she ask me? *Probably because you live across the street, Jerkus,* I told myself.

"Sure, I've got mine in here," I said. "Come up."

I could have brought the book down to her, but I wanted Robin to see my special hideaway, even in its current condition. She bravely started up the ladder. Chloe shook her head and huffed off.

I took Robin's soft hand, carefully helping her ever so gently through the jagged windowpane and inside the attic.

"I have some rain boots that—" I started to say. She stepped ankle-deep into the water. "You can borrow."

I thought I really blew it. I was waiting for her to get furious. One thing I *do* know about girls is that they care more about their clothes—especially their shoes—than anything else.

"They'll dry," she said nonchalantly.

"Sorry. Got sort of a swamp thing going on here," I said.

"Got sort of a yuck thing going on your face," she said, staring at the purple paste still on my face.

I had just won the Loser of the Year award. "It was an experiment. I was trying to—"

"This is amazing," she said, looking around the lab.

"*Was* amazing," I sighed. "The storm smashed the window, then the rain blew in and wrecked everything."

Robin ambled around, studying all my stuff.

I turned from her and used my pajama top to wipe the purple off my face.

She stopped in front of the Thomas Edison poster. "Edison was good, but you should have Benjamin Franklin up there, too. He invented the lightning rod, bifocals, the wood-burning stove—"

"And swim fins," I added. "We could use a pair of those in here."

She panned her eyes to the Thomas Jefferson poster. "Jefferson's face is on a nickel," she stated. "And if you built a column of nickels eight feet high, the stack would be worth three-hundred and eighty-four dollars."

"Jefferson is also on the two dollar bill." I noticed that fact before the blender diced the bill as an ingredient in my failed anti-shaving brew.

Robin sauntered over to Nixon's cage. "You have a California Kingsnake!"

"Don't be afraid," I said. "He's not poisonous."

"I love snakes!" she said. "I also love football—*playing* it, not watching it—chopping wood, and doing the rope climb. Woman hath no limits."

"Woman hath no limits," Echo squawked.

"Who said that?" Robin asked.

"Shakespeare?" I guessed.

"No. I mean just now."

"Oh, Echo, my parrot. She's the world's smartest and some-times most obnoxious bird."

"She's beautiful!" Robin gushed.

"You can feed her," I said, handing her a stalk of celery.

Robin placed the celery into Echo's enclosure and Echo nibbled at it. They both cackled.

"Did you know that it takes more calories to eat a piece of celery than the celery has in it to begin with?" I said.

She ignored me.

"Same with apples," I perkily offered.

"So, what do you do up here?" Robin asked.

I had to think about my answer. "I dream."

"What do you dream about?"

"I dream about everything." (Including her, which I didn't say.)

I held up the steel blender. "In here was my special formula. I can tell you about it now. It's no longer a secret."

"You've been trying to invent a solution to shaving," she said. "Right?"

"How did you know?"

"You hinted at it the other day."

I liked that she was a good listener.

"Last night, I conducted my final test. Had I succeeded, I would have been rich and famous. But I failed."

"Is that what you want to be?"

"A failure? No."

"Rich and famous?"

"Yes and yes."

I pulled my history textbook out of my waterproof backpack. "Here," I said, handing her a dry history book. (The subject of history, however, is hardly dry.)

"What's that?"

"Our history book."

"No. *That!*" She was pointing to Taxi.

"Oh, that. That's Taxi the Tortoise, heroic survivor of last night's storm."

"What's on his back?"

"His shell."

"I mean what's *on* his shell?"

"We call it the carapace. It's the top part of . . ." This wasn't going very well. She made me so nervous I couldn't think straight. I wished I were a cool dude. I thought I'd change the topic by wowing her with another one of my random and bizarre bits of information. "Taxis are yellow because it is the most easily seen color from a distance."

"Well, from *this* distance, Taxi has some kind of splotch on his back. And it isn't yellow," she said, crouching down next to him. "It's red. And it looks like fur."

"He's fine. Believe me, turtles don't have fur coats."

"It's a tiny, little red spot."

"There's nothing there."

"I think you need glasses."

Yeah, glasses. That's all I needed to go along with my red hair and freckles to achieve that total dweeb look. I bent down and picked up Taxi. To my amazement, I too noticed a tiny stain on his shell that I hadn't seen before. "You mean this little patch?"

"Yeah."

"It's just dirt." I tried rubbing it off with my pajama top, but the rust colored smudge wouldn't budge.

"Maybe it's mold," Robin said, standing very close to me. "Maybe Taxi's sick."

I liked that Robin was concerned for Taxi. I gently placed him on the lab table and directed light from my gooseneck lamp onto his back. I grabbed my large magnifying glass and examined his shell closer. Robin leaned in, looking through the glass with me. Our heads were almost touching. I could smell her perfume. (The average human nose is capable of distinguishing over ten thousand different odors.) I wondered if she had put perfume on just for me.

"That's hair," Robin said confidently, pointing to the spot.

"Hair? Like real hair?"

"Not *like* real hair. It *is* real hair."

"Can't be," I said with authority.

"Definitely is," she said with certainty.

"Definitely not," I said definitively.

"Feel it."

I moved my finger across the tiny circle of fuzz. It felt thick, firm . . . like bristles. Actually, more like . . . stubble. "Tortoises don't have hair on their shells," I insisted.

"Well, this one does," Robin said flatly.

I examined Taxi's shell again, even more closely. The area of little fibers seemed to be a small plot of red hair follicles. It appeared that hair, *actual* hair, had grown on Taxi's rock-hard shell.

It was inconceivable. Incredible. *Impossible!*

THE TORTOISE AND THE HAIR

Robin and I took turns looking through the magnifying glass a couple of more times. Each time the answer was the same. Taxi had hair on his shell.

"He never had hair before," I said.

"Before what?"

I had to think hard. "Before last night," I said.

"Before the storm?" she asked.

We looked at each other and then at Taxi, whose head peeked out from under his hood, as if to hear us better.

"What did the storm have to do with it?" Robin asked.

"I don't know."

Robin looked down at the water she was standing in. "Maybe Taxi drank some funky rainwater."

"I don't think this happened from the inside out. I think it happened from the outside in," I said.

"Whatever you just said, whatever it is, it's creepy," she said.

"Creepy, creepy," cawed Echo.

I didn't think Robin would ever agree, but I decided to take a big chance. It wasn't like asking her out for a date or anything, but it was close.

"Wanna help me solve the mystery?"

"What mystery?"

"The mystery of the Tortoise and the Hair."

For the first time, a slight smile came to Robin's lips. Deep dimples creased each of her rosy cheeks. Would she accept my offer?

Before she could answer, her cell phone rang. Her ring tone was Michael Jackson's "Beat It." My absolute favorite song.

"Hello, Mom," she said into her phone. "Okay." Robin hung up, turned to me and said, "I have to go home and do my history homework."

I knew Robin Reynolds didn't need any new friends. She had millions of them. But maybe, just maybe, she would consider getting to know me a little bit better. So, I took another chance. A really big chance. "Can you eight back here tonight at meet?" I asked, in some sort of Martian language.

"Excuse me?"

I was so nervous. I tried it again. In English this time. "Can you meet back here tonight at eight?"

She hesitated, but then grabbed my hand, shook it hard and said, "A date at eight."

"A date at eight!" I repeated, like a parrot.

Robin took the history book, climbed down the ladder into my backyard, and ran across the street to her house. I heard her call out, "Parting is such sweet sorrow. *That's* Shakespeare!"

She quoted *Romeo and Juliet*. I was in love.

I took my recharged McCorder, which because of its rubber case had escaped harm from the storm, and spoke into it, "Message to me: first, do *not* have mud on your pj's and purple paste on your face in front of girls. Second: whenever you're afraid of taking a chance, don't be."

I changed out of my muddy pajamas and shaved my purple face. I recovered quickly from my failure to create an anti-shaving cream. Instead, I had become fired up over the prospect of spending more time with my new . . . what do I call her? Associate? Colleague? Friend?

Sometimes I think it's better not to tell my parents certain things that might upset them. So I didn't say anything about Taxi growing what appeared to be hair fibers. They would ask too many questions . . . freak out . . . quarantine Taxi . . . and get the garage fumigated. Poppy taught me that *silence is sometimes the best answer*.

Before telling anyone about our discovery, I had to make sure that Taxi's hair was real. Then, find out where the hair came from. Then, figure out what to do about it.

At dinner that night, Chloe—as always—led the conversation. "How's your girlfriend and pass the pepper."

"Morgan has a girlfriend?" Dad asked.

"She's a friend, who happens to be a girl," I clarified.

"Who Morgan happened to invite into the attic," Chloe said, trying to embarrass me.

My mom looked up. Before she could say anything, I injected, "She's helping me with an experiment."

"Experimenting in the attic. Sounds innocent enough to me," Chloe said sarcastically.

"Our relationship is strictly intellectual." I knew that would put a stop to any further speculation or inquiries. I added, under my breath, "She's coming back after dinner."

"Experimenting after dark?" Chloe remarked. "Sounds strictly suspicious."

She couldn't leave it alone. Dad was about to send her to her room, but instead asked me, "Is Taxi okay?"

"Why?" I asked nervously.

"I just saw him in the garden. He seemed wiped out from his ordeal last night."

"He's just shy. He has to come out of his shell," Chloe said, McCracking herself up.

"Did you notice anything else?" I asked Dad tentatively. We locked eyes. I couldn't tell if he had seen the patch of red fuzz.

"No," he said.

I felt relieved, until Poppy said, "I did." I turned toward Poppy. "There was something unusual about his shell."

"Like what?" Mom asked.

"It seemed shinier than normal," Poppy said.

"Every part of his shell?" I asked, hesitantly.

"Yep. It was so polished I could see my reflection."

"And Taxi could see *his* reflection in your bald head!" Chloe said.

Everyone laughed except me.

After drying the dinner dishes, I dashed to the backyard to check on Taxi. Sure enough, his furry spot had totally vanished! Not a single hair remained. His shell was smooth and slick, like the fuzz had never happened. How could this be? I rushed Taxi up to the lab for further inspection.

A HAIR-RAISING FORMULA

I had finished draining all of the rainwater out of the attic window through a garden hose. I had repaired most everything inside the *McFactory* and put everything back in its place. I nailed chicken wire over the broken window until we could get a new pane of glass installed. And I patched a gash in the ceiling with a tarp where most of the water had poured in. I also re-attached my posters to the wall and fixed the trapdoor.

As I was spraying aftershave around the lab to freshen the air, I took my McCorder out of my pocket and switched it on. "Message to me: Don't forget to—" Robin's face appeared at the top of the trapdoor, right on time.

"Don't forget to what?" she said.

"Don't forget to . . . I forgot."

"Were you talking to yourself, Morgan?"

"No. I was talking to my recorder. I call it my McCorder. It's how I remember things, like what I just forgot." Whenever I was around Robin, I became instantly stupid—a colossal dork.

"Wow, you cleaned up," she said, looking around from the top of the stairs.

"I showered and shaved."

"I meant your lab," she said, stepping into the *McFactory*, carrying a Tupperware box covered in tin foil.

"What's that?" I asked.

"I made some chocolate chip cookies."

"I love chocolate chip cookies. But they have to be eaten with milk," I said.

My mini-fridge just happened to be stocked with a carton of milk. I grabbed two sterilized stainless steel beakers, which worked perfectly for cups.

I threw some sheets of bubble wrap over the wet couch. We sat down. It sounded like the Fourth of July under our rumps! Sitting there next to each other felt as if we were on a real date, even though I had never been on a real date. After a few awkward moments of listening to the plastic bubbles pop, I raised my beaker and said, "Hair today, gone tomorrow." And I clinked her beaker.

"What kind of toast is that?" Robin asked.

"Taxi's gone bald," I said.

"What?"

"He lost his little patch of hair."

"Completely?"

"Bald as a baby's butt."

"What does that mean?"

"It means babies don't have hair on their butts."

"I mean *why* did Taxi lose his hair?"

"I don't know. I don't know how he got hair in the first place and I don't know how he lost it in the second place." I walked to my lab table and picked up a digital memory card. "But the answers should have been on this," I said. "Whatever happened to Taxi in here last night would have been recorded."

I pointed to a camera lens encased in the rafters above, hidden inside the "O" of the element, H_2O. "It's from my security camera. It captures picture, but not sound," I said. "My gas generator switches on when the power unexpectedly shuts off, like it did last night."

"So we're on television right now? Cool," she said, waving to the camera.

"It records *everything* around the clock. Except last night a hole in the roof sent water rushing onto the camera and soaked the memory card inside."

"H_2O. Such irony . . ."

"I can dry my camera in a bucket of uncooked rice, but the card won't play back."

"A little water shouldn't hurt a memory card. Cutting it in half . . . now *that* would destroy all the data." Robin said, joining me at the lab table.

"Do you have a hair dryer up here?" Robin asked, lifting the card from my hand.

"I have *everything* up here," I declared.

I retrieved a blow dryer from my junk trunk. Robin plugged it in, turned it on, and patiently passed the hot air over the card, front and back. I wondered whether she had attempted this technique on her history book or if she used her wet book as an excuse to see me. While I was engaged in hopeful thinking, she started to sing the song "Jimmy Crack Corn."

"If Jimmy cracks corn and no one cares, why is there a song about him?" I asked.

Robin just looked at me. She must have thought I was a real doofus. "Harriet Stern invented the portable hair dryer in 1962," she said casually.

"Walmart, Kmart, and Target started in 1962," I said.

"Walmart is the largest company in the history of the world," she said.

It was like playing facts ping-pong. I had surely found my *factoidal* soul mate. After a couple minutes, she turned off the hair dryer and handed me the flash card. "Now try it."

I inserted the card into the laptop and this time the video images were there!

"It worked!" I said.

"Told ya," Robin said.

"Told ya!" Echo said. "Woman hath no limits!"

"Behave yourself," I said to Echo.

"Behave *yourself!*" Echo shouted back to me.

We could see a shot of me on the monitor preparing my formula from the night before, talking aloud to my pets, my lips moving—though we couldn't hear anything—as I measured each ingredient, pureeing the concoction, and applying the purple cream to my face. The blackboard was in plain sight, showing my latest formula clearly written out.

I played the video at double speed. We watched me leave the lab for the night and, in the glow of the nightlight, we saw Taxi sleeping on the floor under my stool. I fast-forwarded at triple speed. We saw a flash of lightning followed by the moment the electricity went out, plunging the *McFactory* into darkness. That's when the gas generator would have kicked in, restarting the camera. I continued fast-forwarding, seeing only a black screen.

Just as I was about to stop the video, we saw another flash of lightning on the monitor, which illuminated the entire attic. I resumed playing the video at normal speed. A bolt of white lightning burst into the lab, shattering the glass, blowing out the entire window!

Robin and I jumped back. We kept watching the screen, transfixed as a sparkling electrical current zipped around the *McFactory*. The current lit up the lab, allowing us to watch the wind and rain stream in through the blasted out window, drenching the room, blowing things off the shelves and flipping over furniture, including my stool. It was like an F5 tornado had formed inside the attic. (Each year, about a thousand tornadoes touch down in the United States, far more than in any other country.)

The electric current continued to travel throughout the lab, just missing Echo. I was grateful that her cage wasn't made of metal, or else Echo would have been one fried bird. Taxi huddled on the floor under my fallen stool. The electricity surged along the edge of the lab table, up and down the metal file cabinets, onto the tabletop. It zigzagged across the beakers, over the bell jars, and flickered in and out of the funnels and flasks, blazing through the test tubes and balance scales, busting the top off my big steel blender, diving *inside*, zapping the purple potion and causing it to boil. And turn red.

"That's my anti-shaving formula!" I exclaimed.

We saw the solution in the blender bubble, and a single dollop of bright red liquid erupt from the blender and fall directly onto Taxi's solid shell! *Splat!*

Then, everything on the video went dark again. We kept watching, but the storm had passed and the lightning no longer illuminated the room. The screen was black.

I pushed "stop." Neither of us spoke. My legs started to tremble as I slowly realized that, although I failed to invent the solution to shaving, the lightning bolt from the storm may have caused the exact *opposite* to take place inside the blender, reversing the results. Instead of *preventing* facial hair from growing, I may have accidentally stumbled across the formula for *growing* hair!

Goodbye impossible.

Hello miracle!

FaMe, FoRtUne, AnD FRUSTRaTInG GIRLS

I took the flash card out and placed it on the table. It no longer felt as if Robin and I were strangers. We had just witnessed an amazing occurrence together. Robin peered into the blender.

"You made a whole batch?"

"Yeah," was all I could say.

"There's enough in here to try the experiment again," she said.

"Uh-huh."

More silence.

"Maybe it was a fluke," she said.

"Maybe," I said.

"Maybe," Echo chirped.

Robin and I just looked at each other, wondering what it meant if it *wasn't* a fluke.

"You should test it again on Taxi," she said.

"Right."

"You should see if one drop is enough."

"Okay."

"Try two. Or three. Or more."

"Multiple drops. Got it."

"Or if it needs to be applied every few hours . . . to keep working . . . to keep the hair growing . . . like watering grass."

"Re-apply it. Grass. Right."

"You should put some of your formula on *other* surfaces, too."

"Other surfaces?"

"Just to see what happens."

"Alright."

"I mean maybe it only works when it comes in contact with tortoise shell. Or, on the other hand—"

"What's on the other hand?" I asked.

"Maybe it can work on anything."

"Anything?"

"Anything."

"Is there an echo in here?" I asked.

"Aye, aye, Matey!" Echo answered.

"Like wood, bricks, steel . . ." Robin continued.

"Hair on bricks," I said. "Yeah, that's just what I want for Christmas." I picked up the blender, handling it delicately, like it was a human heart ready for transplant. I inched carefully toward the mini-fridge, being careful not to trip.

"What's your problem with hair on bricks?" Robin asked.

"When was the last time you were at the mall shopping for hairy bricks?"

Robin plopped down on the couch. A couple plastic bubbles popped.

I stopped at the fridge and turned to her. "Robin . . ."

"What?"

"We can't tell anyone about this."

"We?"

"Do you know what our discovery could mean?"

"Our?"

"The two of us could be—"

"Us?"

"Yes! We, our, us." I said. "If you hadn't seen that spot on Taxi, I would never have known about it, especially because it disappeared. I would've given up being an inventor. I would've continued running away from Buckholtz. We're like partners. I owe all this to you."

"Owe what?"

As I placed the blender gently in the refrigerator, I said, "If this secret potion really grows hair on anything—"

"That's a super-sized *if*," she said.

"We don't need it to grow on wood or bricks or steel."

"You said 'we' again."

I closed the refrigerator door, took a deep breath, and walked over to her. "We just need it to grow on a human."

"You keep saying 'we.'"

"Do you have any idea how many people will pay for hair? And how *much* they'll pay for it?"

"People?" Robin asked. "What people?"

I sat next to her on the popping couch and spelled it out for her, one letter at a time. "B-A-L-D people."

Robin and I were closer than ever. I could feel her breath. I thought she might be happy enough to hug me. Or, better yet, kiss me. She looked into my eyes and, after a long silence, said, "I think I should leave now."

"What? Why?" I stuttered.

"Well, you solved the mystery. You found out what you wanted to know. You discovered how Taxi got hair."

"*We*," I said. "We did that together!"

She stood up and headed toward the trapdoor. I followed her, determined to make her stay. "Wait. You can't leave now," I said. "The two of us could be—"

"Good night," she said.

"But, what if . . ." Actually, I didn't know what I was going to say after that. I just didn't want her to go.

"What if what, Morgan?" Robin said, as she stepped onto the attic ladder.

"What if . . ." I swallowed hard. "What if . . . it's the . . ."

"The *what*, Morgan?"

"The cure to baldness?" I whispered.

She thought for a moment. "Then I suppose you'd get what you want."

I just looked at her.

"Rich and famous," she said, before descending the stairs into the garage, walking down the driveway, and returning to her home across the street without a glance back.

Girls! I wished they came with instruction manuals.

HUMAN TRIALS

I watched out my lab window until Robin went into her house and shut the door.

What was going on in her mind? Couldn't she see the possibilities of a hair-growing business? How could she not understand that this could be a historic scientific advancement—that together, we could become bazillionaires?

I knew I had to conduct further tests of my formula (which I named simply *Hair Today*), to prove it was what I hoped it was. I filled a lipstick-sized plastic vial with my special red formula. I attached the vial to a leather strap and wore it around my neck.

I placed five drops of *Hair Today* from my vial onto Taxi's shell. And, following Robin's suggestion, I placed drops where nobody could see them: one on the bottom of our dining room table, one on a cinder block inside our fireplace, and one on the back bumper of Dad's old Jeep. Wood, brick, steel.

As I was going downstairs to bed, I heard a noise that sounded like an outboard motor coming from the den. Poppy was in there snoring loudly. He'd fallen asleep on the couch in front of the television. He still had his reading glasses on and the newspaper in his hand, opened to the want ads. I stared at his bald head.

I was tempted to squeeze a drop of my solution from my vial on top of his shiny head. But I decided to wait until my other test results were in before trying the formula on humans, just in case there were any peculiar reactions.

I turned off the TV, covered Poppy with a quilt, and tiptoed away.

I set my alarm clock for 5:00 a.m. so that I would wake before anyone else. The moment my eyes opened, I bolted upstairs to check on my various "control studies." I found Taxi outside munching on a leaf. I picked him up and inspected his back carefully. Once again, he had developed a very small patch of red hair on his shell!

I darted to the dining room and dived under the table where Kitten Kaboodle, our Calico cat, was playing with a long strand of red hair. It was one of many that had grown out of the wood. The strands looked like stalactites. Each hair was nearly six feet long! I made note of my findings on the McCorder. "Message to me: hair grows longer and faster on wood than on shell."

I looked inside our fireplace at the test brick. It, too, was covered with long, red hair. Really long hair—thirty feet long! "Message to me: hair grows *much* longer and *much* faster on brick than on wood."

Finally, I ran to the driveway and examined the back bumper of Dad's Jeep. Red hair was hanging from the steel like a bunch of "Just Married" streamers. The hair stretched from the driveway to the street—a good hundred feet! "Message to me: hair grows much, *much* longer and faster on metal than on brick."

I cut all the hair from the table, fireplace and Jeep and hid it in the *McFactory's* iron safe for further analysis. Now I *really* wondered how human skin would respond to my formula. But dad was honking the car horn. He was ready to drive us to school. Experiments on people would just have to wait.

In the car, Chloe said she heard that Buckholtz had recovered from his bout with mononucleosis and was returning to class that very day. "Better start running, little brother," she said. I shuddered and clutched the vial around my neck, hoping it would ward off evil spirits.

"Has that Buckholtz kid been picking on you again?" my dad asked.

I didn't want to burden my father. He had enough on his mind. So I merely said, "Buckholtz? No way. He's a wimp."

"I read that his father was arrested for getting into another bar fight," Dad said.

"Setting a fine example for his son," Chloe said.

"Well, let me know if that kid gives you any trouble," Dad said, as he pulled the Jeep up to the school.

Oh, right. Like telling on Brad Buckholtz was going to make my life easier.

To lighten the mood, I fired off a fabulous fact. "Did you know that the sentence, 'The quick brown fox jumps over the lazy dog,' uses every letter in the alphabet?"

It didn't work. I was scared beyond words.

Beyond facts.

First period was geometry. With ten minutes left to the hour, Mrs. Constantine roamed the room, teaching us about trapezoids. The classroom door opened and a slightly pallid Buckholtz aimlessly wandered in. Mrs. Constantine stopped her lecture and stared at him. Over the years, he had failed her course more than once.

Buckholtz started to improvise a rap song, "C'mon, Teach, first day back, cut some slack. Been so sick, been so down, but look out folks, Bucky's back in town." He snapped his fingers, spun around, and took a clunky bow.

"Find a seat," Mrs. Constantine said, unmoved. Buckholtz took his time as everyone watched him mosey to the back of the room and slump into an empty chair, right next to me. As Mrs. Constantine continued her trapezoid speech, Buckholtz leaned over and whispered, "Did you miss me, Hairy-boy?"

Chills vibrated throughout my body. I knew he couldn't hurt me as long as Mrs. Constantine was there. Even so, I said nothing.

"I missed *you*," Buckholtz said.

When Mrs. Constantine had her back turned and was writing on the board, Buckholtz grabbed my arm. "Hairy-boy, did you hear what's happening after school today? You know, in celebration of my return?"

I kept looking straight ahead. A couple random facts quickly came to mind: The penguin is the only bird that can swim but not fly. It would take about 1,200,000 mosquitoes to fully drain the average human body of blood. And no president of the United States was an only child.

"You're getting a free shave," he said, squeezing my arm harder. "I owe you one. Remember? And I always pay my debts."

I felt sick to my stomach. I felt like 1,200,000 mosquitoes had fully drained my body of blood. I felt dead. Buckholtz stretched out in his chair. "I'm going to shave your face *and* I'm going to shave your head. Won't that be fun, Hairy?" He flashed a smile and flashed electric clippers from under his windbreaker. Then he closed his eyes. To compose myself, I flashed on more arbitrary facts: Your tongue is the only muscle in your body that is attached at only one end . . . snails can sleep for three years without eating . . . elephants are the only mammals that can't jump . . . and if NASA sent Echo into space, she would soon die; she needs gravity to swallow.

Mrs. Constantine finished writing her long question on the board: *What is the area of a trapezoid if its height is ten feet and the length of one of its bases is three times the length of the other base, which is four feet?*

"You have until the bell to work out the answer," Mrs. Constantine said, before sitting down to grade papers.

With his eyes still closed, Buckholtz turned to me and said in a low voice, "Hairy, when you get that answer, slide it over. Until then, don't disturb me. I'm napping."

"Bradley!" yelled Mrs. Constantine. "No talking!" She returned to her grading and Buckholtz immediately fell asleep.

My skin was clammy and my insides were turning. There was no way I was going to get scalped that day. I tried to think coolly and logically. I knew that one more spiffy statistic would calm my nerves: nine out of every ten living things live in the ocean. I promptly felt better.

I had established that Buckholtz picked on me because he was jealous of my facial hair. Therefore, what if *he* suddenly grew some? Would he stop teasing me then?

Poppy had said I needed to use my noggin against Buckholtz. Well, I decided to use something in addition to good old McCracken brainpower. I would use my secret weapon: *Hair Today*. It was time to test my special formula on a human.

16

THE BURLY BEARDED BULLY

uckholtz was in a deep slumber. His body sprawled in his seat, his arms dangling by his sides. I saw that Mrs. Constantine was focused on her work and everyone else was fully engaged in figuring out the area of the trapezoid. Meanwhile, I was about to set a little "trap"-ezoid of my own.

When no one was looking, I squeezed a drop of formula from my plastic vial onto each fingertip of Buckholtz's left hand. I observed him carefully. He wasn't waking up, not even stirring. And then, using the eraser of my pencil, I lightly tickled his jaw, cheeks, and chin.

He instinctively moved his hand to his face, as if to swat a fly. Without ever waking, he scratched the itchy areas, rubbing the moist formula from his fingertips into the skin on his face.

If the lotion were to work on a human, I wondered how long it would take before hair would sprout. I didn't have to wonder long. There, before my eyes, I witnessed an astonishing sight: tiny nubs—real whiskers!—began to grow on Buckholtz's big face . . . and on the end of his stubby fingers! It was like watching time-lapse photography as the red nubs grew into short bristles. Red bristles. Real live hair! This was epic!

Within seconds, Buckholtz had a five o'clock shadow on his face. Then the school bell rang.

"Time!" Mrs. Constantine called out. "Pencils down. Papers in."

Buckholtz jolted awake. He turned to me. "What're you looking at, Hairy?"

"Uh . . ."

"Uh, what, Hairy? And where's my trapezoid answer?"

I glanced at the board and immediately came up with the answer. "Eighty feet squared," I whispered to Buckholtz.

"That better be right," he threatened, scribbling down the answer.

Mrs. Constantine rose from her chair and said loudly, "Hand in your paper on the way out. Make sure your name is on it."

We stood in the back of the line, heading up the aisle toward Mrs. Constantine's desk. Then, just for the fun of it, Buckholtz grabbed my vial, ripped the strap off my neck, and spiked it onto the floor.

"Oops. Your girly necklace fell off," Buckholtz barked. "What're you going to do about it?"

I picked it up, retied the leather strap, and put it back around my neck. I was shaking with fear and fury. I felt a fact-attack coming on. My brain went into auto-pilot: Reno, Nevada is west of Los Angeles, California . . . there are more nerve cells in the human brain than there are stars in the Milky Way . . . when the following sentence is read in reverse, it gives you the same sentence: *Was it a car or a cat I saw?*

"You're a chicken, Hairy," Buckholtz said. "After school I'm pluckin' your feathers. And this time you ain't flappin' away."

He flung his paper on Mrs. Constantine's desk and left the room, laughing.

I didn't want to miss seeing the moment Buckholtz found out about his fresh furry face, so I rushed down the hall to catch up to him, being careful to stay a few steps behind while heading across campus.

I could see kids coming toward us, becoming aware of Buckholtz's new facial hair. Their eyes widened. Their mouths dropped open. Some girls giggled into their hands. Buckholtz was starting to feel self-conscious, probably wondering if he had a piece of breakfast caught between his teeth (which he did) or if his zipper was down (which it was).

It wasn't long before he ducked into the boy's restroom. (The average person goes to the bathroom six times a day.) I followed him partway in, hiding in the doorway as he trotted to the mirror. He picked a piece of bacon from between his two front teeth. He pulled up his zipper. He was about to leave when he noticed something else. He leaned into the mirror for a closer look and was stunned by what he saw: new red hair on his face . . . to go with the old black hair on his head. A two-toned man. His hands rose slowly to his cheeks; his fingers stroked his beard for the first time. He was so baffled by the sudden change that he didn't notice the little hairs, which had also grown on his fingertips.

Nor did he notice me slipping out the door.

SNOLLYGOSTER SYNDROME

The cafeteria was noisy and crowded. Robin was eating at a table surrounded, as always, by her girlfriends. They were all talking loudly, each competing for Robin's attention. They dressed like Robin. They talked like Robin. It was clear they wanted to be like Robin—and to be *liked* by Robin.

I sat down at an empty table nearby. She knew I was there but didn't bother talking to me or even acknowledging my presence.

I waited until each of Robin's posse, one by one, bused their dirty dishes to the kitchen area, leaving Robin alone—a rare sight. I quickly picked up my lunch tray, moved to Robin's table, and sat across from her. We were alone.

"It wasn't a fluke," I said.

Robin wiped the corners of her mouth with a napkin.

"I ran some more tests like you said," I yelped, trying to contain my excitement.

She looked away.

"Hair grew on Taxi again."

She pushed her chicken salad around her plate.

"And on wood."

She smoothed her blouse.

"And on brick."

She finished her drink.

"And on steel."

She picked up her tray, stood, and took a step to leave.

"And on *Buckholtz*," I said, revealing the vial around my neck. "I brought some drops to school."

Robin scowled, her eyes finally meeting mine.

"Fact: it takes more muscles to frown than to smile," I said. "So, enjoy the news. And smile." She remained silent, but maintained eye contact.

"Humans, Robin. It works on *humans!*" She slowly sat back down, expressionless. "If you consider Buckholtz a human," I added. She wasn't amused. "I haven't figured out the right dosage or how long it lasts, but *Hair Today* is here to stay! Hey, *Hair Today is Hair to Stay*. Not a bad advertising slogan, is it?"

As Robin was digesting all this along with her chicken salad, Buckholtz plunked down next to me with a thump. I thought the chair was going to collapse. Jerry and Donald, his idiot friends, stood behind him. They were like bodyguards, except without the muscles. Buckholtz still had his facial hair, but I could see that it was beginning to disappear. Note to self: it appears that the *Hair Today* lotion needs to be applied in greater quantity or be reapplied frequently in order for it to last longer on humans. Further testing is required.

Buckholtz put his nose an inch from mine. We were eye to eye. I swallowed and remembered this fact: a person's eyes are always the same size from birth, but noses and ears never stop growing.

"Look at me, Hairy," he said. "See anything different on my face?"

"It's whiskery," I said, hoping his facial hair would last at least through our conversation. "You're no longer the only one man enough to grow a beard around here," Buckholtz bragged.

"So I guess that means—"

"No, Hairy. I always keep my promises, remember? I'm still going to shave you after gym. And I'm still gonna throw in a free buzz cut while I'm at it." He leaned across the lunch table and jutted his prickly chin in Robin's face, "Go ahead, touch it."

Robin didn't even flinch. "A beard doesn't make you a man any more than picking on someone makes you a man," she said.

I couldn't believe my ears. Did she really say that? To Brad Buckholtz's blotchy face? Robin was one brave lady.

Buckholtz blinked once and rose to his feet, puffing up his chest. "I'll see you girls later."

My blood pressure soared and I felt my hands begin to sweat. Buckholtz turned to go, when Robin caught his attention. "I read that mononucleosis can have some nasty after effects," she said.

Buckholtz halted, turned and looked at me. "What's she blabbering about?"

Robin continued, "Just when you think you've recovered, strange things start happening to your body."

"Just be pretty. Don't try to be brainy, too," he said to her.

"It happened to my cousin," Robin said, her lip curled. I could tell she was steaming. But she kept her cool.

"What happened?" Buckholtz demanded.

"You don't want to know," she said.

"Tell me!" Buckholtz hollered, sitting back down.

"It's rare. Don't worry about it," she said.

Buckholtz was becoming more and more agitated. Robin was running out of ideas. She desperately looked to me. I pitched in.

"Yeah, really rare," I said. "They say it only occurs in nine out of eight cases."

"What occurs in nine out of eight cases?" Buckholtz yelled, his face turning cherry red with anger.

"It's called . . ." Robin calmly began, and then gestured to me to take over.

"It's called the Snollygoster Syndrome," I said, making something up on the spot. ("Snollygoster" is a real word. It's a person who can't be trusted. At that moment, that person was me.)

"The what?" Buckholtz asked.

"Snolly," Robin said. "From the Latin, meaning . . ." She turned to me.

"It means 'extremely,'" I said.

"And 'goster' from the Greek, meaning . . ." Robin said, turning to me again.

"Fatal," I said quickly.

"Extremely fatal," Robin proclaimed, trying not to smile. "It's a well-known syndrome."

"You guys are snolly nuts," Buckholtz said.

"Look it up," I said. "PMP. Post Mono Phenomenon."

Robin wasn't done either. She was determined to scare Buckholtz. "Hair starts to grow—" Robin began.

"Yeah? I like that," Buckholtz said, proudly fondling his new stubble with his newly hairy fingers.

"Hair. That you can't *stop* growing," I added without hesitation.

"I wouldn't mind a beard, I guess," he said.

"You'll have a beard you'll never forget. It starts on the face, and then before you know it—" Robin said.

"Think of an ape," I said.

"Boom! Hair starts spreading all over," Robin said.

"Everywhere," I said.

"Even on the bottom of your feet," Robin said.

"Until your toes rot off. Fatal Feet Syndrome," I said.

Buckholtz stood up, processing the information, absent-mindedly fiddling with the hair nubs on his fingertips.

"Oh, and it's also highly contagious," I said. "But only the flesh-eating part, so don't worry."

Donald the Dope and Jerry the Jerk immediately jumped away from Buckholtz. They stared at him, waiting for his response. Buckholtz shook his huge head back and forth. "Yeah, sure. I'm going to turn into King Kong." He leaned back and howled with laughter. Only then did Don and Jerry howl with laughter. Suddenly, Buckholtz stopped howling and slammed his big hands onto my little shoulders, driving me deep into my chair. "See you after school, Hairy." He took out of his pocket electric clippers. And switched them on. "It's gonna be real *goster*. You know—fatal." He and his goons turned and swaggered off.

The chilling buzzing sound of the clippers faded away.

Robin and I sat there, watching them walk out of the lunchroom. She looked at me and asked, "Are you okay?"

I couldn't speak. I hoped that she couldn't see that my hands were shaking.

She tried to calm me down. "Have you heard any good facts lately?"

"Forty is the only number that has its letters in alphabetical order," I managed to say.

"Oh. Well, the number one is the only number with its letters in reverse alphabetical order," Robin returned.

"Four is the only number whose number of letters in the name equals the number," I said.

We sat there a moment. "Do you feel better now?" Robin asked.

"Yeah. Thanks."

I'd call her awesome, but everybody calls everything awesome. Let's just say she was . . . Rob-in-describable.

"About the beast . . ." she started.

"Buckholtz?"

"You know what you have to do, right?"

"I think so," I said.

Robin and I understood each another, without having to talk. That's pretty cool.

"It's your only chance," she said.

I nodded. I remembered that message to myself: *whenever you're afraid of taking a chance, don't be.*

We sat there silently until the bell rang. Those left in the cafeteria got up and hustled to class.

As I got ready to go, Robin touched my arm and said, "*Bonne chance*, Morgan." She strolled off, her ponytail bobbing side to side.

Fact: "*Bonne chance*" means "good luck" in French.

Fact: French toast and french fries aren't French inventions.

Fact: I was falling deeper in *amour* with Robin.

18

GOT SOME SATISFACTION

It was after gym class, last period. Most of the guys had finished dressing and were milling around outside waiting for the last bell of the day. I was dressed, too. But I was hiding inside the locker room, inside the dirty towel sack. It was damp, and it smelled like, well, dirty towels. Other than me, Buckholtz was the last one there.

"Buckholtz!" Coach Gonzalez yelled from the doorway. "Hurry up!"

Buckholtz couldn't hear the coach. He was still taking a shower, singing "I Can't Get No Satisfaction," off-key and at the top of his lungs. I crawled out of the stinky sack and sneaked down the slippery cement floor toward the open shower area, stopping just outside Buckholtz's sight.

When he began washing his hair and had his eyes closed, I stepped forward. He couldn't hear me over the sound of the shower. With my house key, I very carefully pried the top off the soap dispenser and emptied my vial of *Hair Today* into it.

With soapsuds all over his face, with his eyes squeezed shut, with his shrill singing reverberating off the tile, Buckholtz reached out, patting the air in search of more soap and just missed touching me. His fingers found the dispenser on the wall. He depressed the button several times until his palm was filled with a mixture of the school's liquid soap gel and gobs of my secret formula. I sneaked around the corner and crouched behind a waist-high wall.

He scrubbed his face and "cleaned" his entire body, slathering his arms, torso, legs, and feet. (I was pretty nervous. That must be why I remembered that an eight-minute shower uses seventeen gallons of water. And that it takes seven and a half years for the average American residence to use the same amount of water that flows over the Niagara Falls in one second.)

And then it happened. *Hair Today* took root. Instantly, bright red hair started popping out on his chest, on his back, on his sides. Everywhere, if you know what I mean. I had to keep myself from laughing.

Buckholtz stopped singing and stopped moving. His hands froze in midair, as he realized something felt different, something seemed wrong, something strange was happening to him. He stroked his arms and could feel long, shaggy hair. He rubbed his legs and could feel long, bushy hair. Off his butt a tiny tail was forming! He immediately rinsed the soap from his face so that he could open his eyes, which had six-inch lashes! And when he looked down at himself, he couldn't believe what he saw—every square inch of his skin was covered with thick, wild red hair!

I quietly exited the locker room, wandering out of the gym, listening to the screams coming from the shower room. A traumatized Buckholtz wouldn't be bothering me that day after school. He'd messed with the wrong Hairy-boy!

I walked cheerfully and safely home, without anyone chasing me, without losing one whisker off my face, without losing one hair off my head.

Finally, I got some satisfaction.

After dinner that night, I ran across the street and knocked on Robin's front door. She opened it. And looked me over. "No black eyes. That's a good sign," she said.

"Buckholtz never laid a hairy finger on me."

"That Post Mono Phenomenon can be miserable, they say."

"He got a bad case. With some gnarly side effects." I smiled. "And front effects, back effects and— "

"I get the picture."

"The formula worked again. Perfectly. Buckholtz turned into an enormous Elmo right in front of my eyes!" I said. "I felt so . . . powerful."

"I'm happy for you."

"For *us*. We stand to make a fortune!"

"Off other people's *mis*fortune!"

"What?"

"Men can't help it if they're bald," she said.

"Now they can. We're going to sell them hair."

"It's just hair!"

"Which is just what they want!"

She stepped out onto the porch and shut the door behind her. She looked around, and then, after a moment, she said, "Do you want to know what really bothers me—what keeps me up at night?"

"I sure do."

"I've never told anybody this." Robin looked away.

I couldn't believe she was about to confide in me.

She simply said, "I wonder who my real friends are."

"Why?"

"Because I'm not sure if they like me for what I look like or what I act like."

"Really?"

"When we first met, you said you liked my ponytail."

"Yeah. I still do."

"You don't get it. You just don't get it."

"Get what?"

"Get who I am."

"Of course I get who you are. Uh, I think," I said not very smoothly. "What does this have to do with our formula?"

"*Your* formula," she volleyed back.

"But we're partners," I said.

"No, we're not. We're not even friends."

She stormed back inside her house, slammed the door, and left me to figure out what the heck she was talking about. Not even friends?

Girls. I swear, what's with them?

19

WARNING: DON'T DIS MY DAD

The next morning, Poppy was in the living room reading the *Carlsbad Courier*. He held it up so I could see the front page. There was a large photograph of Buckholtz, his body covered in red shaggy hair. The caption read, "Local Boy Has Bad Hair Day."

"It's dangerous out there," Poppy said. "They spotted Bigfoot near your school."

"I'll be careful," I said, with a slight grin.

"I wonder how that happened." Poppy folded the paper, took off his reading glasses, and scratched his head. "How's that no-more-shaving invention coming along?" he asked.

"It's no more. Didn't work out as I had planned," I said.

"That happens sometimes. You start in one place and end up somewhere altogether different," he said, looking at the picture of Buckholtz. "Sometimes better," Poppy added. "You know, 'different' can be 'better.'"

"Yeah, maybe it's better."

I grabbed my backpack, getting ready to go to school.

"It's okay, Sparky," Poppy said. "Even though I could sleep in a little longer if I didn't have to shave, shaving is part of my morning routine. It wakes me up. Refreshes me. Gives me a chance to look myself in the face—ten minutes to stare into the mirror and reflect. That's time well spent." Poppy always looked on the bright side. He struggled out of his reclining chair and wobbled into the kitchen. I followed him.

"Poppy?"

"What?"

I hesitated, then asked, "What if you could grow hair again?"

"You're always thinking, aren't you?"

"Wouldn't you like to look younger? Get those jobs you want."

Poppy poured himself a cup of coffee (the most popular beverage in the world) and said, "Not having hair. I've gotten used to it. It's who I am—a bald guy."

"But if you could be an un-bald guy, a guy with a full head of hair," I said, "wouldn't you like that more?"

Chloe scurried through the kitchen, grabbing a banana on her way. "Hurry up. Dad's already in the car," she said before flying out the door.

Poppy put his coffee cup down, rubbed his bald skull, and smiled. "Hair on my head? Humm. I'd have to spend time washing it, drying it, combing it, cutting it. I'd have to spend money on combs, shampoos, conditioners, haircuts. I don't know, kid. At my age, hair seems more like a bother than a benefit."

I watched Poppy return to the living room. He sank into his chair and perused the job listings in the newspaper.

As I was leaving the house, he called out, "Whoever turned Buckholtz into a grizzly bear was using his brain."

When our Jeep pulled up to school, we saw several television cameras, news journalists, and radio reporters gathered on the front steps. In the middle of the media mayhem was Buckholtz. His new unwanted hair had "evaporated" overnight. Jerry and Don were planted on either side of him like the lion statues at the New York Public Library. (At the time it opened in 1911, the library was the largest marble building ever constructed in the United States.)

"What's all this?" Dad asked.

"Buckholtz is a celebrity," Chloe said. "He ran around in a red gorilla suit yesterday."

"Yeah. Except it wasn't a suit," I murmured.

Chloe and I got out of the Jeep, said good-bye to Dad, and ran up the stairs to the front doors, which were obstructed by reporters.

"Mr. Buckholtz!" one of the journalists shouted out, "Do you have any idea how you suddenly grew all that hair?"

"Nope," Buckholtz answered, relishing the attention.

Another reporter asked, "Do you have any idea how you suddenly lost all that hair?"

"Nope."

"Do you think it will happen again?" another reporter asked.

"It better not," Buckholtz said, spotting me in the crowd. "Or something really bad is going to happen!"

He didn't scare me. Because in my pocket was my vial. I had reloaded it the night before with *Hair Today*. I was armed and dangerous.

Chloe fired a question of her own, "Mr. Buckholtz, do you think you'll ever graduate?"

Jerry and Don laughed until Buckholtz threw them a harsh look. The reporters tried to ask more questions, but the morning bell rang and the crowd slowly dispersed. Chloe ran ahead to class. I got as far as the lobby before Buckholtz stepped in front of me, blocking my path.

"Hello, Hairy," he said, with his cretin pals by his side.

"Hi," I mumbled.

"Side effect from mononucleosis? Hair attacks? Fatal foot disease?" Buckholtz snarled. "I looked it up, my mom looked it up, my doctor looked it up. You *made* it up. And now, guess what? I'm going to *beat* you up!"

Just before he could make a move toward me, Mr. Palimaro, the principal, breezed by and said, "Ten minutes. Get to class, boys."

Buckholtz waited for Mr. Palimaro to pass before saying, "After school. My fist, your face. Wanna bet which one will win, Hairyboy?" Buckholtz laughed, then he and his two losers walked off.

His fist would win against my face. No question. But still, it was time for me to stand up to him. I only hoped my noggin' and my vial of *Hair Today* would be strong enough to put an end, once and for all, to this barbarian's threats. I took a deep breath, then called out, "Yes!"

Buckholtz whirled around, "What?"

"Yes. I want to bet."

"Don't waste my time."

"I bet your fist won't beat my face," I said, wishing my voice sounded a little tougher. Or lower.

"Oh, really?"

"Because there won't be a fight." I stated.

"Are you a fortune teller now?"

"Sorry. No fight."

I admit my pulse rate was climbing. I thought about some of my favorite factoids: Ninety percent of people have an innie belly button . . . there are 293 ways to make change for a dollar . . . the average life span of a major league baseball is seven pitches . . . a dime has 118 ridges around its edge. When I felt relaxed and ready, I said, "So, wanna bet?"

Buckholtz slowly retraced his steps back to me. "You'd never bet," he said.

"Wanna bet I'd never bet?"

"Okay. What's your big bet, Hairy? A penny?"

"How does two thousand pennies sound? Twenty dollars that there won't be a fight," I said, praying that my plan would work.

Jerry and Don gasped.

Buckholtz continued. "You're in for a rough day, Hairy. Not only are you going to lose a fight, you're going to lose, let's say *thirty* bucks."

Jerry and Don looked at each other, excited over how much Buckholtz had increased the wager.

"Forty," I countered.

"Fifty!" Buckholtz shot back.

Fifty dollars was a lot of money. I had never bet on anything before. This was getting out of hand. I felt myself crumbling. I didn't have fifty dollars.

"I knew you wouldn't go through with it. Where would you get fifty dollars? I hear your old man doesn't have a nickel!" Buckholtz shouted.

They all laughed.

My blood started to boil. Nobody makes fun of my dad!

"Okay. Not fifty," I said.

"I knew you would fold. See you at your funeral, Hairy. Three o'clock sharp." He turned to leave.

I plunged my hands into my pockets. "Make it an even hundred," I said.

Buckholtz spun around. "One hundred dollars? Really, Hairy? You're willing to lose that much that easily?"

"No."

"I didn't think so."

"I'm looking forward to *winning* a hundred dollars. From you." I popped the stopper out of the vial in my pocket with my thumb and squeezed a large quantity of *Hair Today* into my right hand, "One hundred bucks, Holtz!"

I removed my hand from my pocket and reached it out to Buckholtz to seal the deal, keeping my palm down so that he wouldn't see the red goo smeared on the inside of my hand.

THE AFTER-SCHOOL FIGHT
THAT NEVER WAS

Buckholtz glared at me while the Dopey Brothers stood behind him with their mouths wide open. "If we fight, I win one hundred dollars. If we don't fight, you win one hundred dollars," Buckholtz said. "That's your measly bet?"

"Unless you want to keep going higher, which I'd be happy to do." For a moment my heart stopped. I stood with my hand outstretched, waiting for him to shake on the deal.

Buckholtz turned to his friends. "You heard him, right?" His friends just nodded, impressed—as I was—at the amount at stake.

"There's gonna be a fight. I'm gonna win the fight. I'm gonna win one hundred dollars!" Buckholtz said.

"Who *wouldn't* take that bet?" Don said to Jerry.

"It's a no-brainer," Jerry said to Don.

"Bring it on!" Buckholtz said, grabbing my hand as hard as he could. He knew his grip was hurting me. But, what he didn't realize was that the force of his grasp was transferring my formula deep into the skin of both of our hands.

"It's a deal," I said, feeling slightly faint.

"Sucker," Buckholtz sneered. He removed his hand from mine, turned, and strutted down the hall. His friends hustled behind, like ducklings. I furiously wiped the goop off my hand onto my jeans. Then I wondered if *Hair Today* would grow on denim.

"Oh, one more thing," I said, calling after him.

Buckholtz and his clowns stopped and turned around.

"If you ever threaten or bother me again—"

"Yeah, Hairy? What're you going to do?"

"I'm going to do my voodoo on you. That's what I'm going to do . . . do."

Buckholtz walked back to me, raised his massive arm and cocked his fat fist like he was going to slug me. I didn't back up, I didn't back down. For the first time, I didn't run. I simply placed my hands in my pockets and smiled, waiting for the big surprise.

"At one second after three o'clock, your face will look like a crushed watermelon, Hairy," Buckholtz said with his fist still clenched in front of my face.

"My name is Morgan. *You're* hairy," I said.

At that glorious moment, red hair started flowing out between the knuckles in Buckholtz's fist. He and his bonehead pals turned white. Hair kept spraying out of his palm. Buckholtz screamed and jumped around. He tried to shake the hair off, like his hand was on fire.

"It's happening again!" he squealed.

"Can you say *Morgan*?" I asked him coolly.

"What have you done to me, Hairy?" he shrieked.

"This is just the beginning," I said. "And my name is Morgan."

Buckholtz was horror-struck, his eyes fixed on the hair oozing from inside his hand. "You're the one who did this to me yesterday!" he accused, watching the spaghetti-like hair crawl all over his fingers.

"Unless you leave me and every other kid in this school alone," I said to his terrified face, "I'll turn you into a giant red fur ball again! And *next* time it will be permanent!"

"No!" he pleaded.

"Or I might shrink you to two inches tall."

"Don't— "

"Or make farts come out your ears."

"No!"

"I can do anything I want to you. It's my voodoo!"

"Help me! Somebody help me!"

"Still want to fight today?"

Hair, lots and lots of hair, kept growing out of his hand. He had had enough. "Stop it! Stop it now!" Buckholtz screamed.

"No name-calling, no threatening, no chasing, no betting, no fighting. Got it?" I said.

"Yes!" he shrieked. "Yes! Yes!"

I pulled my hands out of my pocket and pointed *my* hairy finger at Buckholtz and bellowed, "Now, WHAT'S MY NAME?"

Buckholtz looked at my hairy hand and nearly passed out. "Where did you come from?" he whimpered, convinced that I was a mad mutant, some alien from outer space.

"Boston. Home of America's first subway. NOW SAY MY NAME!" I yelled.

Buckholtz despised being humiliated in front of his buddies, but he slowly started to stammer, "Mor—Mor— Mor . . ."

"Do you really want hair growing out your eye sockets?" I warned.

"Mor—Morg—Morgan," he sputtered.

"ONCE MORE!"

"Morgan," he growled.

"I can't hear you!"

"MORGAN!" he blared.

Goliath had been defeated. He was near tears.

"Never call me 'Hairy' again. And never EVER say anything about my dad again! Do you understand?" I said.

He nodded meekly.

He deserved a knockout punch. "Swear!" I demanded.

"I swear."

I let that sink in. Morgan McCracken had spoken. The enemy had surrendered. The war had been won. I walked briskly past Buckholtz down the hallway to my class. I'd never felt better.

Steadying himself against the lockers was a reporter from the *Carlsbad Courier*. He had witnessed everything. And looked like he had seen a ghost.

It was three o'clock. The final bell had rung. School was over. Outside the gym, Buckholtz, Don, and Jerry silently stepped aside as I sauntered past them. I noticed that the hair on Buckholtz's hand was still there, but had stopped growing. The hair on my hand was gone. I documented my findings into the McCorder, "Message to me: The formula reacts differently on different people and on different body parts. Oh, and *Hair Today* doesn't work on denim."

I wanted to tell Robin about Buckholtz—about my latest findings and my latest conquest—but she wasn't talking to me. I wondered if anything could bring us back together.

THE BALD AND THE BEAUTIFUL

When I reached the end of our block, I saw about a hundred people standing in front of our house. I encountered a police barricade. "Sorry, son," said Officer Hernandez, a stubby motorcycle cop. "I can't let anyone else in."

"What's going on?"

"Some kid in that house invented hair."

"Hey," I said. "That's *my* house. That kid is me!"

Officer Hernandez looked me over and decided to lift the yellow caution ribbon, allowing me to duck under. I saw a long procession of men in the center of the street leading to my front door. The men had one thing in common: they were all bald.

Clustered on our front yard were more news crews and reporters than had been at school that morning. As I got closer to my home, I saw my dad, my mom, Chloe, and Poppy on the front porch trying to answer questions from the press.

"This is the first we've heard of this," my dad said.

A radio reporter shouted out, "Mrs. McCracken, do you have any idea how much your son's invention will be worth?"

"All we know is that Morgan loves to tinker," Mom said.

Another reporter yelled, "Chloe McCracken, do you—"

"That's spelled C-H-L—" Chloe said, before another reporter poked a microphone in Poppy's face and asked, "Is your grandson going to test his formula on you?"

Poppy pointed me out in the crowd and replied, "Ask him. He's the man of the hour!"

All the cameras swiveled toward me. The line of bald men began to hoot and holler. Suddenly, a group of journalists surrounded me. I was packed in so tightly that I couldn't raise my hands to scratch my nose. (A woman's nose can detect more scents than a man's can.) A camera was shoved in my face and the female reporter asked, "Morgan, can you really cure all these men of baldness?" Before I could answer, there was a barrage of more questions from the other reporters: "Which cosmetic company has bought your invention?" "What will you do with all your money?" "Will you quit school?" "Will you *buy* your school?"

"No comment! No comment!" I yelled. I had seen politicians say that on television. They were usually being led away in hand-cuffs at the time.

I put my head down and wiggled through the throng to the front porch to stand with my family. I raised my hands above my head to quiet the crowd. They gradually grew still.

By now, the column of bald men had grown, stretching clear down the block. They were of all ages and types. Some wore suits. Some wore shorts. Some had round heads, some had flat heads, and some had pinheads. They all had glossy, bare heads. I recognized Mayor Michelson. And Principal Palimaro. And Reverend Reilly. They were looking at me with hope in their eyes . . . and cash in their hands.

I stood tall and addressed the assembly. "*Stewardesses* is the longest word you can type using only the left hand. With the right hand, it's *lollipop*," I said. Everyone stared back at me, in disbelief. "We're sorry. We have nothing more to say at this time. We must ask for your patience and our privacy." Celebrities always refer to themselves as "we." "We thank you for coming," we concluded.

The news people groused and began to break up. "But, to the gentlemen in line . . . wait here," I said. Then, I opened the front door to my home, turned to my family on the porch, and whispered the words, "*We* need help!"

The First Rule of the McCracken Manor was that anyone at any time could call for a Family Summit. The Summits are for a member of the family to discuss a problem or make announcements that would affect all of us. And so, the moment we entered the house, I called for an emergency Family Summit.

We sat in the living room. I quickly described how my hair discovery came about, how I was trying to invent a solution to shaving, how a lightning strike changed the chemical properties of my experiment, how Robin pointed out the hair follicles on Taxi, how I used the formula against Buckholtz, and how he would never bother me or any other student again.

"If nothing else," I said, "*Hair Today* solved my bully problem. The other goal I wanted to achieve," I turned to my parents, "was to invent something that would be a big seller, so that you would never have to worry about money again."

My father stood up, walked around the room, and then spoke. "There are a lot of men outside asking for your help. Wanting your attention. Needing your formula. You shouldn't keep them waiting." He paced back and forth like a commander inspecting his troops. "Your mother works hard. She likes her job and earns a fair salary." He gestured toward Poppy. "Grandpa wants to work again, and he will. He likes to work, whether it's for money or not."

Dad stopped in front of me. "And I'm going to get a job again." He took a moment to collect his thoughts. "I appreciate that you want to pitch in, Morgan, but I promise you, we're going to be fine. All of us. No matter what. We're McCrackens." He looked deep into my eyes. "Do what you enjoy doing, but don't do it for money. And certainly don't do it for me."

Everything got quiet. After a moment, Mom said, "Your formula's a great accomplishment, Morgan."

Poppy said, "We're very proud of you."

Chloe asked, "Will you buy me a car?"

Poppy laughed his big-belly laugh, releasing the tension in the room. And a small fart. We all burst into laughter.

"I'm still in the testing phase for my product," I told them. Everyone looked at me, wondering what I was going to do. "So, well, I better get out there and continue testing," I said.

TOWN OF REDHEADS

I brought my blender down from the lab and stayed on my front porch until dark, doling out what the bald men called their "dream come true."

I made clear to them that the formula was only good short term; that when it was manufactured they would have to use it every day; that this was just a sample of things to come; that I would create more in the coming weeks; that very soon they would have forever what they thought they could never have again: hair. Real, live, healthy, growing hair. And red hair, at that! We were going to be a town of redheads! (About 1 to 2 percent of the population of the world has red hair.)

I wouldn't accept any money. I figured this was a good chance to research my product on different scalps and a good opportunity for the men to experience having hair again, if only for a brief time. I recorded the characteristics of each man and how much *Hair Today* I gave to them, as this was my first group study.

I dug into the blender, scooping out *Hair Today*, smearing the hair-raising substance onto the bald heads of friends, neighbors, and strangers. I wore latex gloves so that the formula wouldn't touch my hands and grow hair on my fingers again.

After I massaged the last man's head, Officer Hernandez rolled up the yellow caution tape. Before he left, he bashfully approached me.

"I lost my hair at the age of twenty-three," he said. He removed his helmet, knelt and presented his hairless head before me. I felt like I was knighting him as I rubbed *Hair Today* onto his barren dome. He said, "Bless you," put his helmet back on, and zoomed off on his motorcycle, leaving me on my front porch on my first night of fame. On the eve of great personal prosperity. Alone. Except for a dozen scattered red whiskers growing on my latex gloves.

I saw the drapes being pulled closed in Robin's window. I wondered what was going through her mind. I wished I could share all this with her. I wished I could convince her to make hair with me.

Poppy opened the front door and said, "It's getting late." He drifted outside and looked up at the sky. "Ah, a night full of stars."

He sat down on the top step of the front porch and drew in a deep breath. "You are one of them today, Sparky. A real star."

"Thanks, Poppy," I said.

I sat down next to him, admiring the night sky. "If you tried to count all the stars in our galaxy at a rate of one every second, it would take around three thousand years," I said.

"That puts us in our place, doesn't it?" Poppy said.

I noticed a black stretch limousine parked in front of Robin's house. The tinted window in the backseat was slightly open, out of which I could see smoke from a cigarette waft into the night.

"So, how did it go out here?" Poppy asked.

"Good. They'll all have hair tonight. But they may not by tomorrow. It doesn't last."

"Nothing does. That's what makes the present so precious."

I turned to Poppy. He was looking up at the heavens. "You miss Grandma, don't you?"

"I'd do anything to have one minute back with her."

"I wish I could invent a time machine for you."

"Start working on that, will ya?" Poppy had tears pooling in his eyes. "There's a wise, old Irish saying—"

"Wait," I said, as I took out my McCorder. I switched it on. "Go ahead, Poppy."

"*Love is the only thing . . . and everything.* One day you'll understand that," Poppy sniffed. "You'll do anything for the person you love."

I looked up at Robin's window and wondered if the feelings I felt for her were love. They must have been, because I would've done anything for her.

I picked up the blender of *Hair Today*. "I have a couple drops left," I said.

"Nah," Poppy said. "Thanks anyway."

"Why not? It'll make you look younger."

"I'm not younger. No matter what I look like."

"But maybe they'll hire you if they think . . ."

"I wouldn't want to work for someone who doesn't want to work with somebody my age."

We both just sat there, listening to the crickets. (By the way, female crickets do not chirp.) After a few moments, Poppy asked, "Have you protected the idea?"

"What do you mean?"

"The formula. Have you registered it with anyone official? Or taken out a patent or anything?"

"Gee. No. Not yet."

"Without a patent, you can't prove it's your idea. If someone got their hands on your formula and took out a patent before you . . ." He looked off. "Well, you wouldn't want that to happen." Poppy stood up. "Let's go in. It's time for dinner."

When he opened the front door, Poppy turned to me, pointing to my blender. "Do you have any mustaches in there? I'd take one of those."

I smiled. "One mustache coming up!" I coated my finger with the last of the formula and ran it across Poppy's philtrum, over his top lip, under his bulbous nose.

"In all my years, I've never had the patience to grow a mustache," Poppy chuckled and went inside the house. (McStachtoids: In a deck of cards, the King of Hearts is the only King *without* a mustache. Since William Taft in 1909, all US presidents have been clean-shaven. Some people call mustaches "mo's," "caterpillars," or "crumb catchers.")

I heard a car engine turn on and saw the limousine on the other side of the street begin to move. Its headlights remained off as it crept suspiciously out of the cul-de-sac, the cigarette smoke lingering behind.

I followed Poppy into the house and locked the door.

MILLION-DOLLAR MIRACLE MIXTURE

It was 3:26 a.m. There was loud rapping on the front door of our house. Mom turned on the lights as my whole family gathered in the foyer and groggily staggered toward the doorway. Our next-door neighbor's dog was barking loudly.

"What's going on?" I asked.

"I don't know. But I don't like visitors in the middle of the night," Dad said.

Chloe was the first to notice that Poppy had grown a thick, red handlebar mustache overnight. "Lookin' pretty hip, Poppy-pops," she said.

Poppy stroked his new mo. "I got a good deal. I know the inventor," he said.

My father stood at the front door and cautiously looked through the peep hole. "Yes?" Dad said.

"My good man, is this the McCracken household?" a male voice with a British accent asked.

"Yes, who are you?"

"I'm from Johnson & Myers, the pharmaceutical company. I'm here to talk about the miracle mixture."

"At this hour?" Dad said.

"We've been traveling all night," the man said. "We wanted to be the first to make a proposal."

My dad opened the door. Three men stood there under the porch light, each wearing a pinstriped suit and each holding a stainless steel briefcase. We could see a taxicab waiting at the curb, its motor idling. The tallest man spoke for the group. "First of all, I wish to apologize for coming so early. It appears we may have awakened you," he said, his breath visible in the cold night air.

"Is anything wrong?" my mom asked.

"No, everything's right," the man said with a pleasant smile.

"Nothing's right about three-thirty in the morning." Chloe yawned. (The average yawn lasts six seconds. Seeing, thinking, or reading about yawns can trigger a yawn in 50 percent of people. Have you yawned yet?)

"I don't think you'll mind being up once I tell you why we're here," the Englishman said. He waited to be invited in, but Dad didn't offer.

"My name is Dr. Fredrick H. Duncan. I'm the CEO of J&M," the man continued. Then he looked straight at me. "And you must be the genius inventor everyone's talking about."

"I'm Morgan McCracken. You can call me Morgan."

"Well, this is your lucky day," Dr. Duncan said. "Because today, Morgan, I'm going to give you a ton of money." (A ton of one-dollar bills amounts to $908,000.)

We all looked at each other. Dad said, "Please, come in."

There we were. Five McCrackens. All wearing bathrobes. We sat around the dining room table with the Brits as Poppy served the men tea, sizing each of them up.

One of Dr. Duncan's aides opened his metal briefcase, revealing a bulky, leather-bound book on which was emblazoned, in gold lettering, the word *Contract*. Dr. Duncan began his presentation. "I'll make this fast so you can go back to bed and we can go back to England. Young Mister McCracken here has come up with a nifty little product."

"Little?" Poppy mumbled to himself, twirling his new "mo."

"And I'm here to purchase it outright. Simple as that," Dr. Duncan said, opening the *Contract* to the last page and turning his attention to me. "Sign here, son, and before the ink dries you'll be the richest man in this town."

I looked to my parents. They were looking at each other. I looked at Chloe. She was nodding wildly, like a bobblehead doll. I looked to Poppy. He was just looking back at me.

I didn't know what to do, what to think. I had never been faced with this sort of situation before. It had all happened so fast. My heart started pumping loudly. I tried to calm myself down with these random facts: On the average, sixty-one thousand people are airborne over the United States in any given hour. Marie Curie's notebooks are still radioactive. And Donald Duck never wore pants. But whenever he got out of a shower, he would always put a towel around his waist.

"Uh. Well, it cost me a lot to come up with the right formula," I said, wanting to make sure that I sold *Hair Today* for enough money. "I mean I had to buy a lot of ingredients."

"I'm sure you did," Dr. Duncan said.

"For example, I went through a whole case of Tabasco sauce."

"Tabasco sauce. I see." Dr. Duncan said with a sly grin.

"And I spent a week's allowance on kumquats."

"Well," said Dr. Duncan, "Would one million dollars cover your expenses?"

As we all sat in shock, Dr. Duncan's second assistant swiftly snapped open his briefcase, which contained ten thousand brand new one hundred dollar bills. There on our dinner table—a million bucks. (If you counted one dollar at a time, every second, for twenty-four hours a day, it would take you twelve days to count a million dollars.) My big moment had come. I was one signature away from being a millionaire. (Bill Gates, the richest man in the world, was twenty-four years old when *he* became a millionaire.)

"Immediate prosperity. Immediate fame. Immediate happiness," Dr. Duncan said, guiding the briefcase full of cash across the table to me. "Congratulations, son."

The aide handed me a diamond-encrusted fountain pen and said, "Write your name on the last line, give us the formula, and we'll get out of your hair, so to speak."

Chloe couldn't take her eyes off the money. Mom gave a concerned look to Dad. Dad gave a troubled look to Poppy. Poppy gave a puzzled look to me. I held the pen an inch from the paper. It was heavy. My hand was shaking. (I'm left-handed, just like Babe Ruth, Alexander the Great, and Bart Simpson.) My mouth was dry. (There are more bacteria in your *mouth* than there are people in the world.) My head was spinning. (Your brain is sending and receiving six trillion messages every minute in order to keep your body working right.)

"A million dollars . . ." I said softly.

"You earned it, Morgan McCracken," the aide said.

"That should pay for the kumquats," the other aide added.

"It's a very generous offer," I said.

"I'm sure it will change your life. And that of your family," Dr. Duncan said, adjusting his bowtie.

"One. Million. Dollars," I said, wiping my brow.

"Go ahead now," the Englishman said. "Sign your name, so you can take the money. And start spending it tomorrow."

I began to write my name. Then, after the letter "k" in "McCracken," I hesitated.

"You're doing great, Morgan . . . McCrack," said Dr. Duncan. "Just two more letters, son."

"Give us an *E*! Give us an *N!*" Chloe yelled like a cheerleader.

Just as I was about to finish signing for a million dollars, my hand stopped. Something didn't feel right. I wasn't sure what it was. I lifted the tip of the pen off the paper.

"I can't," I said.

HOOKED LIKE AN EARTHWORM

D r. Duncan and both his aides, sitting at our dining room table, gasped.

Chloe gave a little scream of frustration.

"Surely you know how to write your name," one of the aides said, becoming restless.

"I can't agree to anything until I consult my partner."

"Nobody mentioned anything about a partner," Dr. Duncan said, shifting in his chair, searching his assistants for an answer. They shrugged their shoulders.

"Robin Reynolds, from across the street," I said. "She spotted the fuzz on Taxi."

"Spotted the what on what?" Dr. Duncan was becoming impatient.

"I have to talk with Robin," I said, growing in confidence.

"She isn't your wife," Chloe said. "Just sign the darn contract, so we can be rich! And so we can go back to sleep!"

"Robin's my associate. We have to decide these matters together."

"Associate? She's just a chick you have a crush on," Chloe said.

"She's a friend."

"She's a friend you have the hots for."

"She's smart," I said.

"You mean she's pretty."

"I mean she's pretty smart."

"Then what's she doing hanging with you?"

"She's not anymore!" I didn't know what more to say, except to come up with a fast fact. "Baby robins eat fourteen feet of earthworms every day."

Dr. Duncan rolled his eyes. "Uh, can we—"

"Admit it, Bro," Chloe said. "You're hooked, just like a fisherman's earthworm."

"We have a working relationship," I shot back.

"Like I believe that."

"Like I care."

"Guys, this isn't the time," Dad said.

"Robin's done a lot for me," I said.

"Yeah, up there in your love lab," Chloe said.

"Mom . . ." I whined.

Dr. Duncan couldn't believe what he was hearing in the middle of this life-changing, million-dollar business transaction.

"We'll talk about this later," Mom said.

Dr. Duncan took a deep breath. "I understand. Not a problem. Just run across the street, get your fellow scientist and hurry back.

Both of you sign, both of you split the money, and we'll have our-selves a deal."

He held up the diamond pen. "And if the two of you are back in three minutes, you can keep this pen. It's worth a hundred thousand dollars. Call it a *signing bonus.*"

I got up and started toward the front door, when Dad stood. "It's too early to wake Robin's family," he said. Then he turned to the men. "It's none of my business, Dr. Duncan, but I think we should discuss all this among ourselves and get back to you."

"You're right," Dr. Duncan said, as he rose from the table.

"Thanks," Dad said.

"It's none of your business."

"Well, let me put it to you another way," Dad said. "Morgan isn't signing anything until he's ready."

"He sounds ready to me," Dr. Duncan said. "He just needs his little friend to co-sign."

"We need more time," Dad said. "We won't be pressured into making a decision of this magnitude in the middle of the night . . . in our pajamas, no less."

Dr. Duncan looked Dad up and down, readying himself for a hard-nosed negotiation. "We're flying back to London in two hours, Mr. McCracken. There's no time for further deliberation."

"We wish you a safe flight," Dad said.

"With all due respect, this is the *boy's* invention. This is the *boy's* decision," Dr. Duncan said.

"Morgan is a minor. And he's my son. He—"

"All right," Dr. Duncan interrupted. "I think I know what you're *really* saying—what you're *really* asking for." He slid the third stainless steel briefcase across the table to my dad.

"I simply want everyone to be happy," Dr. Duncan said with a smug smile.

We all looked at Dad. He set his jaw and slid the case back across the table, unopened, to Dr. Duncan. "No, thanks. When it's time, my son will make the right choice. And I'm sure your offer will still stand."

"Wrong. This is my last offer and your last chance to accept it," Dr. Duncan said, popping open the third case and revealing a stack of shiny gold bars. It was like a treasure chest had been unlatched. I heard a choir of angels sing in my head. (Gold is the only metal that doesn't rust.) Dr. Duncan pushed the open case across the table once again to my dad. I just stood there, stunned. Those gold bars must have been worth, well, their weight in gold.

Poppy broke the silence. "Like my son said, we'll think about it." He shut the case, pushed it back to Dr. Duncan. "Sorry, gentlemen."

Dr. Duncan closed the case of gold and the case of cash. "You're making a big mistake. You won't get a better offer. I'll leave my card. When you change your mind—and you will—call me."

Dad held the front door open for the three men, who stormed out without saying another word.

Chloe's face dropped. Mom smiled. Poppy left to wash the teacups. I sank into the couch feeling woozy. The McCracken family had just turned away a bloody fortune.

BAD DECISIONS MAKE
GOOD STORIES

After the men left our house and we were all getting ready to go back to bed, Dad turned to me. "You have to think about what you really want to do with your invention."

"And we'll support whatever decision you make," Mom said.

"But think fast," Poppy said. "Because I have a feeling Morgan McCracken is about to be very popular, very soon."

At that very moment, everything got very chaotic. The phone rang. There was a knock at the front door, a thump on the side door, and banging on the backdoor. All of us, including Kitten Kaboodle, started running in different directions through the house.

"I'll get the phone!" I called out.

"I'll get the backdoor!" Mom said.

"I've got the side door!" Dad said.

"I'll cover the front!" Poppy said.

"I'll be doing my nails," Chloe said.

I grabbed the phone. "Hello," I said.

"I wish to speak to Mr. McCracken," a woman's thin voice said.

"Actually, there are three Mr. McCrackens here—my grandfather, my father, and me."

"I'm looking for the McCracken who can grow hair."

"That's me. I'm like a hair farmer."

"Excellent! Your invention is one of the world's most desired commodities. I'm Asuka Kasumi with Yamamoto International, calling from Tokyo, Japan."

Just then, Mom shouted, "Morgan! There's someone at the backdoor who wants to talk to you! Right now!"

"Miss Kasumi," I said into the phone. "Could you please hold for a second?"

"As you wish, sir," she said. "But don't be long. My five million dollar offer won't wait forever."

I ran to the backdoor with the words "five million dollar offer" reverberating inside my head. Standing there in the dark was a heavyset man smoking a fat cigar and wearing a white three-piece suit and a white ten-gallon cowboy hat. (I don't know why they call it a ten-gallon hat. It only holds six pints.)

"Hi," I said.

"Howdy, partner. And I *do* mean partner. I sure hope you don't get seasick."

"What? Why?"

"Because I'm taking you and your family on my private yacht to Fiji," the man with the southern drawl and red, white, and blue suspenders said. He fished a silver key out of his suit pocket and dangled it in front of my eyes. "And did I mention that the yacht is yours to keep?"

"That's very nice, but—" I said.

"But, you're right—first I'd like to shake the hand of a real mastermind," the man said, grabbing my hand and pumping it too many times. "I'm Colonel Clovis Coleman, the oil tycoon from Houston." (The first word spoken on the moon was "Houston.") "And I'd like to make you a Texas-size proposal for your hairgrowth formula!"

"If you can wait just a minute, I've got somebody holding on the phone," I said.

"I'm sure you're getting other bids, but I want you to know that I'll buy your formula for *twice* what anybody else is willing to pay." He whipped out a blank check. "Just tell me the dollar figure to write on this check. And it's done. No negotiating. No waiting. No fine print."

Just then, Dad yelled, "Morgan! There's someone at the side door that wants to talk to you! Right now!"

"Take your time, son. Because I ain't leaving here without a deal and nobody can beat my offer," the ten-gallon Texan said.

I ran to the side door, yelling to my mom, "Tell the lady on the phone that I'll be right there."

At the side door was a short woman with nervous eyes who wore way too much makeup. Before extending her hand, she licked her fingertip and smoothed down her eyebrows.

"Hello," I said, shaking her limp hand.

"*Bonjour*. I'm Madame Belle La Fleur, president of Hair Care Laboratories, with offices all over the globe." She dampened her eyebrows again and handed me a velvet business card.

"It's very nice to meet you," I said.

"It's a true honor to meet you. I cannot wait to be in the Morgan McCracken business. I'm quite certain you and I will enjoy an extremely profitable future together."

"That's very flattering, but—"

"The brilliant part of your idea is that men have to use it each and every day. If they want to keep their new hair, they have to keep buying the product. And women—they're always looking to thicken their hair. *Hair Today* is a gold mine. Tell me, how did it all come about?"

"One storm. One tortoise. One girl," I said.

"We call that 'One-derful.' And, just think—we'll create Morgan's Hair Products and Accessories, as well. Combs, brushes, scissors, curling irons, shampoos, conditioners, gels—"

"Sounds great."

"—hair dryers, dyes, clippers, trimmers—"

"Wow. It just keeps coming."

"—and hair salons. We'll open a chain of them all over the world!"

"*McCracken's*," I suggested. "Just like McDonald's, but without the fries."

"Do you have any idea what sort of financial empire we'll have?"

Just then, Poppy called out, "Sparky! There's someone at the front door that wants to talk to you! Right now!"

"Miss Madame, can you give me a minute?"

"I've waited for this moment all my life, monsieur. I think I can wait one more minute."

"Thanks."

"Oh. One more thing. I'm prepared to transfer one billion dollars into your bank account right now."

I almost swallowed my tongue.

She sucked her fingertip and flattened her eyebrows again. (On average, people touch their faces nineteen times per hour.)

I ran to the front door, yelling to Mom again, "Tell the lady on the phone that I'll be right there."

I rushed to the front door. "It's your partner, or pal, the fuzz finder," Poppy said, stepping away.

Robin was standing there in the dark, dressed for school, wearing her backpack. And there I was, wearing my pajamas again.

"I'm going to school," she said. "Will you walk with me?"

"It's a little early, isn't it?"

"We need to talk," she said, indicating with her eyes that it was urgent.

I turned to Poppy. "Can you handle everything?"

"Don't worry. I'll say we'll get back to all of them," Poppy replied.

I ran downstairs to change out of my pj's and to get my homework. Something inside told me that leaving the house with Robin before dawn wasn't a good idea. But Poppy always said, *"Bad decisions make good stories."*

DIFFERENT, LIKE BETTER

obin and I walked together. It was still dark outside. She
didn't speak for the longest time. Then, she turned to me
and said, "I just needed to talk to you. Alone. In private."

"We're not going to school?"

"After I've said what I have to say, we can go back home, back
to sleep."

"Okay. So what's on your mind?"

"Those Englishmen came to my house after they left yours."

"Did they offer you money?"

"Oh, yeah. Lots of it. They figured if they got me to sign, then
you would, too."

"Did you sign?"

"First of all, I don't deserve anything for your invention."

"But you were the one who—"

"More importantly, I would never do anything I didn't believe in."

Out of the corner of my eye, I saw the same stretch limousine from earlier that night. It was behind us, driving along the curb very slowly with its headlights off.

"Don't you believe in *Hair Today*?" I asked.

"I believe *Hair Today* could corrupt the world."

"What? How does growing hair on bald men mean the end of civilization?"

"I don't think a man should be judged by how much hair he has."

"Huh?"

Robin held up an imaginary bottle of *Hair Today*. "Attention all bald people. Here's a lotion that will change your life," she said, acting like the host of an infomercial. "Rub it on your head and you will have hair and therefore you'll be better looking and therefore people will like you. *Hair Today*, happiness tomorrow." She stopped walking. "We're born the way we are, Morgan. We should just accept that. We shouldn't care whether someone has hair or doesn't have hair. Some people have red hair and freckles. Doesn't mean they aren't attractive or they should be ashamed of it or change it." She placed her hand on my arm. "I like you, Morgan, not because of your looks."

"You don't like my looks?"

"Of course, I do. But I also like you because you're clever and nice and funny and we're a good team."

I couldn't believe I was hearing those words from Robin. Or that her hand was still on my arm.

"I thought you were different from everyone else. Different in a good way. Different, like better," she said.

I thought about those words, "*different, like better*." She sounded like Poppy. She started walking again, looking away, probably so I wouldn't see the mist filling her eyes. I sneaked a peek at the dark limousine, which was still cruising slowly behind us. I couldn't see through its tinted windows. I was getting worried.

"Ah, Robin—"

She continued to talk. "You're going to make plenty of money from your inventions."

The limo began to speed up.

"Hey, Robin—"

"But I hope you don't sell your soul along the way."

The limo turned on its headlights, the beams lit us up.

"Yo, Robin—"

"Some things are more meaningful than money, Morgan. Like principles!"

"And living!" I yelled.

The limo was headed right for us. I grabbed her hand. "We've got to run!" I said, pointing out the limousine, which was barreling down on us.

"Who are they?" Robin screamed.

"Who cares?" I screamed.

"Why are they after us?"

"Can we talk about that later?"

We fled across the street. I admired her speed. We ran through Poinsettia Park, cutting across the soccer field. The limousine left the street, jumped over the curb and chased after us, its tires chewing up the grass. We ran around the picnic tables, the drinking fountain, and the swings in the playground. But we couldn't get away from that black limo. Birds scattered. Squirrels scampered up trees. Gophers dove into their holes. Fortunately, it was so early in the morning that no people were around to be injured. Or killed.

"This isn't good!" Robin cried out.

"We can hide in the new hotel!" I shouted. "No reservations needed."

"This really isn't good!" Robin cried out louder.

A hotel was under construction just ahead. No workers were there at that hour to help us. But there would be plenty of places to hide. And we'd only need to stay hidden until the construction crew arrived. We hustled across the street. The limo was close behind us, fishtailing, honking its horn and flashing its headlights. (At that life-and-death moment, all I could think was that most American car horns honk in the key of *F*.)

We wiggled through an opening in the fence that surrounded the construction site and charged into the structure. We could hear the limo screech to a stop and a car door slam. ("Screech" is one of the longest one-syllable words in the English language.) I decided to tell Robin that fact later, if we were still living. We hid behind a tall stack of lumber, holding our breath. The sun was beginning to rise.

We heard footsteps. Then a man's intimidating voice, "C'mon, kids. I just wanna talk. I'm not gonna hurt you. I promise."

"What do we do?" Robin asked quietly.

"We just have to stay still," I answered. "He'll never see us."

The man spoke again, sounding nearer than he was a moment earlier. "The longer it takes for me to find you, the crankier I'm going to get."

"He's getting closer," Robin whispered.

"You might as well give up," the man said. "There's no place to go. And, trust me, you don't want to see my cranky side."

"I'll think of something," I whispered to Robin.

"Good. Think. That's what you do best."

The footsteps grew louder, as the man drew nearer.

"I've got an idea!" I said.

27

THE MAN WITH THE BLOODY HATCHET TATTOO

Robin crouched next to me, behind the stack of lumber, our knees touching.

The man kept coming. Kept threatening. "If I find you before you give yourselves up, things will turn very ugly very fast. Now, COME OUT!"

"Anytime, Morgan!" Robin said. "What's your brilliant idea?"

"Well, as you know, I'm an expert in being chased."

"That doesn't make me feel better."

"I've decided that . . ."

"Yes?"

"We should run!" (The word "run" has more definitions—179, to be exact—than any other word in our language.)

I took Robin's hand and pulled her from behind the lumber pile. We rushed toward the lobby area, aiming toward a central staircase. We leaped up the unfinished staircase two steps at a time. We could hear the man chasing after us, huffing and puffing. We kept going up and up the stairs. It was nice having Robin's hand in mine.

We reached the fifth floor. The man was nowhere to be seen behind us. We ran down the hall, trying to pick a room to hide in. But none of the doors had been installed—you could see right in. So we darted to the fire exit at the far end of the hall, burst through the door and dashed up a stairwell until we came to a door marked ROOF. We opened it and found ourselves seven stories above the ground. There was no place else to go. We ducked behind a large air conditioning unit.

"We're safe now, right?" Robin said.

"Very," I said.

Just then, the man emerged through the rooftop door.

"I meant 'not very,'" I said.

The man strode to the far side of the roof looking for us. He was huge, like three hundred pounds. He had a tattoo of a bloody hatchet on his neck. I had to think fast. I grabbed the vial around my neck and squeezed drops of my formula onto the steel guardrail that ran along the perimeter of the roof.

"What are you doing?" Robin asked quietly.

"Hair grew the fastest and the longest on steel," I said. "The metal in this railing has a much higher alloy ratio than the bumper on Dad's Jeep, due to the molecular crystallization of—"

"What's the *plan*, Morgan?"

"We're jumping overboard."

"What?"

"It's Rapunzel time," I said. "Time for a hairy ride."

Hair shot from the steel railing. When the beefy man's back was turned, I said to Robin, "We have to lighten our load." We took off our backpacks and stowed them inside the air conditioning equipment. I grabbed a tuft of newly grown red railing hair and said, "I'll go first, in case—"

"In case of what?"

"In case *you* don't want to go first."

"Will it hold us?"

"You've got to trust hair. It's one of the most durable fibers on the planet. In fact, an entire head of hair can hold twelve tons of weight. And . . . if we don't take the leap now, we'll be hatchet-ed."

"That's not even a word."

I had to prove to her that this would work. I grabbed a thick lock of the hair, apprehensively stepped over the rail, and slowly lowered myself toward the alley far below. I felt like Tarzan swinging from a vine. Now it was Jane's turn.

"Come on!" I said. "It's easy."

Robin peered over the wall. Her face paled. "You're asking me to jump off a cliff!"

"Hold some hair and hop over! And hurry!"

As the massive man began walking toward Robin, she got up the nerve to clutch a handful of new hair and ease herself over the wall. Luckily, the hair was as sturdy as a rope. The rail served as a solid anchor, feeding out new strands every second. As the hair grew, it lowered Robin slowly down the side of the building.

Soon we were hanging next to each other, descending at the same rate of speed. It was clear by the panic-stricken look on Robin's face that she didn't like being suspended eighty feet above the ground, and, at that moment, she didn't like me. As we were slowly dropping, I tried to calm her.

"Did you know that hummingbirds can't walk?" I asked.

"What!" she cried.

"Tiniest bird in the world."

"I don't care!"

"Weighs less than a penny."

"Morgan!"

"I'm just trying to relax you. If you focus on facts, then you won't think about—"

"The fact that I can't hold on much longer?"

"Their little wings flap seventy times a second."

"Stop!" she yelled.

And stop, we did. In midair. The hair stopped growing and we stopped descending. We were dangling twenty feet above the ground, holding on for dear life.

"What happened?" Robin called out.

"We stopped," I said.

"Thanks. Why?"

"I guess we got all the hair those drops were good for."

"Happy landings!" the tattooed man screamed from on top of the roof. His giant head was visible over the ledge above. He had a hunting knife in his hand and was sawing Robin's railing hair.

"Oh, great! A haircut. Now what?" she asked.

"Now we pray," I said.

I looked down and saw a dumpster in the alley directly below us, full of trash and garbage. Someone had thrown an old mattress on top of all the rubbish. "Wow. Way to pray," I said to Robin. "Now, jump! It'll be a soft landing."

"Never!"

"We have no other choice."

"If I die, I'm going to kill you!" she screamed.

It was clear that Robin was terrified. "Used mattresses," I said, "have an estimated ten million dust mites in them."

"Ew!"

"Be grateful. That layer of mites will pad our fall."

She couldn't hold on any longer. She let go of her twine of hair, madly kicking her feet in the air until she tumbled onto the spongy mattress.

The tattooed man began to pull me up the building by my hair—my railing hair, that is.

I opened my hands and dropped, landing right next to Robin, bouncing to a stop.

"Are you okay?" I asked.

"Yes, but I'm not going to stop praying!"

We climbed out of the dumpster and took off running as fast as we could. Just before reaching the end of the alley, Robin yelled triumphantly, "We made it!"

28

ROBIN SAVES THE DAY

The alley led to a busy boulevard. The police station was just around the corner. Robin and I ran as fast as we could. We were moments away from freedom when the black limo crossed in front of us, skidding to a stop and blocking our escape. A muscle-bound driver jumped out from behind the steering wheel. He looked like Shrek in a cheap suit. I thought of grabbing Robin's hand and running back in the direction of the dumpster, but by then the hatchet guy had made his way from the hotel and was coming up behind us. The back door of the limo swung opened and a deep voice from inside bellowed, in no uncertain terms, "Get in!"

I looked at Robin and she nodded. "We have to," she said.

I climbed into the plush backseat after Robin, with my mother's constant warning to never get into a stranger's car ringing in my ears. We were facing the rear of the limo and staring into the one good eye of its passenger—a small, middle-aged man in a velour tracksuit with a jagged scar across his forehead and a patch over his left eye. He looked like a modern-day pirate. Echo would have loved him. He slammed the door, locking us in.

I had never been inside a limousine. It had a TV, a mini-bar, laptop, and sound system. It was so cool. Well, except for being trapped inside with a madman and a monster.

"Are we being kidnapped?" I inquired. "Because that's seriously against the law."

"I ask the questions," said the one-eyed lunatic. "And I have just one. Where's the formula?"

"What formula?" I asked.

"I ask. You answer," he said.

"Why do you want to know?" I asked.

"They said you were intelligent. But there you go asking questions again."

"Tell him," Robin said to me. "So he won't hurt us."

"He's not going to hurt us."

The man withdrew a gun from his belt.

". . . too much," I added. For the first time, I realized how much trouble we were in.

"The formula. Where is it?" he insisted.

"I don't remember," I said.

"You have one minute to remember!" he exploded.

Robin turned to me. "What do you mean you don't remember?"

"The only place I ever wrote it down was on the blackboard."

"So that's where it is," the one-eyed man said.

"No. The storm blew in and washed the chalk off."

"Well, I'm sure you memorized it," Robin said.

"I changed that formula like five times a day. A little something here, a little something there. A pomegranate seed one day, a sprig of rosemary the next. A pinch here, a splash there. A dash of this, a sprinkle of that. A teaspoon of—"

"OKAY. I get the idea!" Robin shouted, starting to freak out again.

"But I didn't memorize it like it was a cake recipe!" I was starting to freak out, too.

The wicked one-eyed man leaned forward. "I know you have the formula. Because without it, you have nothing."

"If I had it, I'd give it to you. If I could remember it, I'd tell it to you," I pleaded.

"I want it NOW!" he belted, pointing the gun straight at me.

"Uh, did you know that every human spent about half an hour as a single cell?" I couldn't help myself. A flood of facts came to mind. I was having a minor nervous breakdown. "A Boeing 747's wingspan is longer than the Wright brothers' first flight. Months that begin on a Sunday always have a Friday the 13th in them. And it's impossible to lick your own elbow. Go ahead. Try."

"You have thirty seconds left." He cocked his gun. "Before this conversation gets messy."

The one-eyed man was right. Without my formula written out, I would never be able to patent it, own it, or profit from it. It suddenly struck me: I had lost everything! All those rich offers from that morning meant nothing.

Also, would this maniac really shoot us if I didn't hand over the formula? This was disastrous!

"Think, Morgan. That's what you do best, so do it!" Robin said in a panic.

"Every ingredient, each exact measurement was on that black-board," I said. "It's gone. It doesn't exist. I don't have it!"

"You must have written it down somewhere else!" Robin screamed.

"I didn't!" I hollered.

"Ten seconds," the one-eyed man said.

"THINK, Morgan!" Robin said.

"I CAN'T think when you're YELLING at me!"

"You're going to get us KILLED!" Robin said.

"Five . . ." the one-eyed man said.

"Did you record the information into your ridiculous McCorder?" Robin asked frantically.

"I forgot to charge the batteries!" I cried out. "And it isn't ridiculous! It helps me to remember—if I remember to charge its batteries."

"Four . . ." the one-eyed man counted down.

"You must have entered the data into your computer?" Robin was getting more and more desperate.

"I was going to, but—"

"Three . . ." the one-eyed man said, ready to pull the trigger.

"USE YOUR HEAD!!!" Robin screamed.

"Two . . ." the one-eyed man said.

"It's NOWHERE!" I yelled.

"ONE!" the one-eyed man screamed.

"THE SECURITY CAMERA!" Robin blurted out, covering her head with both hands, as if that would protect her from taking a bullet point blank.

I looked at her.

The one-eyed man looked at her. "What security camera?" he asked.

"In Morgan's lab. The surveillance camera. It records every move he makes. It will show exactly what Morgan wrote on that blackboard," Robin said.

"Totally! She's brilliant! That's where you'll find my formula. Please don't shoot her—I mean us," I said.

The man paused, lowered his gun and said, "Where's this video?"

"Next to my microscope," I said.

"Where's your microscope?"

"In the *McFactory*," Robin said.

"What the hell is a *McFactory*?"

"My lab," I said.

"Where's your lab?"

"At his house," Robin said.

"WHERE IN HIS HOUSE?" the man was getting more and more impatient.

"Technically, it's not *in* the house. My lab is in the garage. Again, technically it's not *in* the garage, but *above* the garage," I said, becoming more and more jittery. "See, it used to be in the basement—my lab, not the garage—but when Poppy came to live with us, I moved—"

"Shut up!" the one-eyed man said. "Let me get this straight. There's a recording—"

"It's on a flash card," I said. "A digital flash card."

"Okay, a flash card. Next to your microscope. In your lab. At your house. Above the garage."

"You got that perfectly straight," I said.

"On that card—" he said.

"Some people call it an SD card. That stands for Secure Digital—" I was spinning slightly out of control.

"On that card I will see—" he interrupted.

"The formula," Robin said.

"And it's the ONLY record of the formula," he said.

"Unfortunately. I mean yes," I said. Then I added, "A piece of paper cannot be folded in half more than seven times."

"He may have discovered the cure to baldness, but this boy is crazy!" our kidnapper said.

"He's crazy smart," Robin yelled back. I was stunned (and pretty happy) that she would defend me in the middle of this perilous escapade.

Just then, the front door of the limo opened and the huge man with the hatchet tattoo struggled in, taking the seat next to the driver. He didn't look very jolly.

"If that flash card isn't there . . ." the one-eyed man said. "If the formula isn't visible, if you're lying . . ." He never finished his threat. Instead, he roared at the driver, "Back to the house!"

Robin squeezed my hand the entire drive home.

29

MORGAN SAVES THE DAY

It was still early in the morning when the limo came to a stop and parked in my driveway, but our cars were already gone, and no one was at home. Dad must have driven Chloe to school. Mom would be at work by now. Poppy was probably out looking for a job.

The one-eyed man put his gun in my face. "Get the flash card and bring it back to me."

"If you could fold a piece of paper forty-two times, it would reach to the moon," I said.

"NOW!" he said.

"Okay," I said. "Come on, Robin."

The man seized Robin's arm. "When I see your formula all spelled out on the video, then you both can go free. Until then, she stays here," he said, leaning across my body and opening the car door. "Gibson will make sure you don't try anything stupid."

The tattooed guy who'd chased us got out of the car and walked me toward the garage. Every step of the way, I tried to think of something I could do to rescue Robin. I had gotten her into this mess. I had to get her out.

Gibson pushed me into the garage. I unlocked the trapdoor and climbed up the stepladder through the hatch into the *McFactory*. He followed, struggling up the stepladder, barely able to squeeze his wide hips through the narrow opening.

We were greeted by Echo, who squawked, "Ahoy!"

Gibson jumped, fists clenched, ready to fight. "Who said that?" he asked, spinning around.

"My bird."

"Well, tell your bird to shut up."

"Shut up!" Echo repeated.

"Echo, shut your squawk hole," I said.

The flash card was sitting safely on my lab table, next to my microscope. I picked it up and said, "Here's what you want. What everybody wants. It's all there."

"Prove it!" Gibson said.

I inserted the card into my computer and played the video. It showed the interior of the lab as recorded by my security camera, the same footage Robin and I had watched the day after the storm.

Just as Robin had predicted, hatchet man could plainly see the blackboard and every single chalk-written notation for creating *Hair Today*. He could see me on camera, placing every element in the blender, announcing—although there was no audio—each property and its proportions.

I almost cried. I couldn't have made it easier for these thieves. I had to think of something before just handing over my greatest invention. I ejected the card and held it up. "This is it. My formula. The secret to *Hair Today*," I said.

Gibson smiled and said, "Give it to the boss. Let's go!" Then, he pushed me toward the trapdoor.

I needed to neutralize Gibson—take him out of the equation. On my way to the trapdoor, I quietly and inconspicuously kicked open the door to my snake's cage. I stood over the stairway to the garage.

"After you," Gibson said.

Instead of walking down the stepladder, I employed my athletic emergency jump technique, leaping from the attic landing through the opening and onto the cement floor of the garage. I quickly closed and locked the door behind me, trapping Gibson inside. He yelled some swear words I had never heard before. Words I can't repeat. But, of course, Echo repeated them. Several times.

I snatched a pair of gardening clippers, sneaked around to the side of the garage, and laid the ladder leading to the window down on the grass.

Gibson ripped the chicken wire off of the side window, leaned out and screamed, "Put that ladder back!"

I heard Echo say, "Shut up!"

Gibson immediately got on his cell phone and shouted into it, "Get up here! I'm about to be attacked by a poisonous serpent! Help!"

I smiled, knowing that Nixon had done his job.

I scampered to the driveway and stood in front of the limo, holding up my flash card. The one-eyed man stepped out of the car. He was on his cell phone talking to hatchet man. After a moment, he hung up.

"That was Gibson. He says the video shows the formula. That's the good news. Bad news? You locked him in the attic with a killer snake. He's deathly afraid of snakes. That wasn't very nice."

"Let Robin go or I'll do something even not nicer. I'll *destroy* the formula," I said, realizing that I *would* do anything for her.

"You're not going to destroy something that's worth billions of dollars," he said. "Now bring it here."

"Not until you release Robin," I said boldly, even though I thought I was going to piss my pants.

"This isn't a game, little boy," he said. "Just give me the card and I'll give you your girlfriend."

"He's not my boyfriend," Robin said. "We're just . . . neighbors."

"Hand it over," he said to me.

"You first," I said like a gunslinger in a black and white cowboy movie. "And to set the record straight, we're not just neighbors, we're partners. Sure, I was hoping we could become more than—"

"NOW!" he yelled.

The muscular limo driver opened his door and stepped out. Robin screamed from inside the limo, "Give it to him, Morgan!"

It was time for a relaxing fact: A giraffe can clean its ears with its twenty-one-inch tongue. I felt much calmer. But then, the driver started moving toward me. That's when I held up the pruning shears. "One more step and I'll slice this card in half, wiping out all the information forever." The driver stopped in his tracks.

"As dumb as you are, you're not *that* dumb," the one-eyed man said.

"Hey, give me credit. I was dumb enough not to make a copy of the formula and dumb enough not to patent it. Now, let Robin go."

"When I have the card, I'll free her," he countered.

"I'm calling the shots here," I said, not backing down. It was the all-new and improved Morgan McCracken. "When I have Robin, I'll give you the card."

It was a standoff, like playing chicken with our lives. Well, Robin's life.

"MORGAN! Don't do this!" Robin shrieked.

"She's not leaving this car—certainly not alive—until I have that formula in my hands," the man announced. He raised his gun, aiming at my chest.

I placed the flash card inside the blades of my gardening clippers. "Let her go right now or I'll cut the card. It's your turn to have thirty seconds," I said.

He started to squirm. "I don't believe you," he said.

"Fine. You have twenty-five seconds more not to believe me."

"You're bluffing," he said.

"Twenty-four," I said.

"MORGAN!" Robin yelled.

"Listen, punk—" he said.

"Tick, tick, tick," I said.

Finally, the man yanked Robin out of the limousine and shoved her toward me.

"Okay, hand it over," he said.

Robin ran to my side. I flung the card to the one-eyed man who caught it. Without delay, he eagerly inserted it into the limo's laptop. Robin and I gradually backed away. This was our chance to escape.

She was holding my arm tightly. "We could have been killed back there," she whispered.

"Yeah, that would have sucked," I said. We turned and started speed walking.

She looked into my eyes. "You gave up your formula for me."

ECHO SAVES THE DAY, SAVES THE DAY

"Not so fast." The limo driver grabbed us by the back of our necks and shoved us into the garage. "Open it!" he said, indicating the attic door.

I unlocked the trapdoor and lowered the stepladder. Gibson was standing above us in the attic with his arms folded, fuming. He wiggled his broad body through the narrow hatch, maneuvering his fat feet down the stairs. When he reached us, he gestured toward the attic.

"Get up there!" he said, withdrawing his hunting knife.

Robin and I swiftly climbed the stepladder into the lab. Gibson slammed and locked the door behind us. We had traded positions with Gibson, but at least we were feeling safe, especially when we heard the limousine speed away.

"Oh, this is great. Just great. School is about to start and we're stuck up here," Robin said.

"We were just abducted! And almost murdered! And they stole my—our—invention! And you're worried that you—we—might be a little tardy to Spanish!"

"*Sí*. Now, please call the police. They'll get us down from here, arrest those guys, and get your flash card back. *Comprendes?*" Robin said.

"Good plan. But my cell phone is in my backpack. Where's yours?" I said, scooping up Nixon and returning him to his cage.

"In my backpack," she said.

"And where are our backpacks?"

"On the hotel roof," she said, realizing our dilemma.

"So much for calling the police or anyone else," I said.

"So we're trapped?"

"*Sí*. And they've run off with my—our—formula."

"Formula," Echo yelped.

"Shush, Echo," I said, turning to Robin. "And they'll register it with the patent office under their name."

"Formula," Echo said again. I disregarded her. "I'll be left with nothing. Zero, zip, zilch. Not even a smidgen left of my best invention ever."

"Smidgen—" Echo said.

"Echo, I'm not telling you again. Zip your beak!"

"—of rubber cement," Echo cheerfully chirped.

"Did you hear me?" I exclaimed. I turned to Robin, "Sometimes she can be so stubborn."

"Dash of mud," Echo said.

"Echo, stop!" I said.

"*Dash of mud*? What's she talking about?" Robin said.

"Ignore her. She's just showing off," I said.

"Dab of comb honey," Echo said.

"Honey?" Robin said.

"Did you just call me 'honey?'" I said.

"She's trying to tell us something."

Gradually, it dawned on me. We walked slowly to Echo. My heart started to race. I opened her cage door and gently placed her on my index finger and brought her up to my nose.

"Echo, did you—" I said.

"Broccoli stem," Echo said.

"Memorize—" Robin said.

"Squirt of maple syrup," Echo said.

"The entire—" I said.

"Quarter-tube of toothpaste," Echo said.

"Formula?" Robin and I said together.

"Half-cup of buttermilk, squeeze of kumquat, three egg yolks . . ."

To our amazement, Echo continued to rattle off each and every ingredient and exact measurement of the *Hair Today* formula. She had committed to memory every word I had said when I was mixing the formula together on the night of the storm. Robin intensely jotted everything Echo was saying onto a small piece of scrap paper.

"Echo," I said. "I love you!"

Echo continued reciting the formula until she tweeted the final ingredient, "Stick of cinnamon."

"You're incredible!" I yelled.

"Woman hath no limits," Echo crowed.

Robin finished writing down the formula and handed me the slip of paper. "There. You have your formula back," she said.

"Blend it all for thirty-three seconds and—" I said.

"And don't forget to catch lightning in a bottle a second time," Robin quipped.

You'd think I would be ecstatic. But I returned Echo to her cage and slumped onto my stool.

"What's wrong? Now you'll be rich and famous," Robin said.

"It's too late. I'll never beat them to the patent office."

"You had the formula first. It is clearly your invention. It's been all over the news," she said.

"Those guys will just say I stole it from them and tried to take the credit. And I won't be able to prove them wrong." I stood up. "Robin, we've got to get that flash card back before they register the idea as their own!"

"*You've* got to get it back. I've got to get to school," Robin said, walking to the side window. She looked down through the torn chicken wire and saw that the extension ladder was lying on the ground. "Oh, poop. We're still trapped."

"Poop," said Echo.

"Watch your language, Echo," I said, joining Robin at the window. "Please don't go. If you leave now, we may never—"

"Poop," Echo said again.

I walked over to Echo's cage.

She looked right at me, and again said, "Poop, poop, poop!"

"What do you mean, Echo?" I asked.

"Storm," Echo said.

"Yeah?"

"Scared," Echo said.

"And?"

"Poop!" Echo said.

"You pooped?"

162

"Poop. Ingredient. Formula." Echo said, poking her beak out the bottom of her cage, indicating the lab table below.

Robin and I looked at each other, dumbfounded. I tried to figure out what Echo was trying to communicate.

"Are you saying that the storm scared you so much that you pooped, and your poop dropped through the hole in the bottom of your cage into the blender?" I asked.

"Aye, aye, Matey!" Echo sang out proudly.

This was extraordinary news! *Gross* news, but *great* news. Not only had my formula been preserved, but it also included a top-secret, one-of-a-kind component that nobody would ever figure out: parrot poop! Echo's parrot poop. I turned to Robin. "Stay with me," I implored. "We'll copyright the poop version of the formula and buy our own limo!" ("*Uncopyrightable*" is the longest word in the English language that doesn't repeat a letter.)

"Do you have a bed sheet or anything I can lower myself down with?" she asked, looking out the window at a ten-foot fall. "Or a drop of *Hair Today* I could put on the wood windowsill?"

"They've got the card, but they don't have the formula!"

"Just one drop should do it."

"And without the right formula, their patent will be worthless!"

"I've told you where I stand on this, Morgan. Do what you have to do. But I'm doing what I have to do. I'm going to school. So, please grow me some hair to climb down on."

"Robin—"

"Thanks for saving my life and everything. But I want out of here. Now!"

I reluctantly went to my *In Case of Fire* cabinet and withdrew an emergency rope ladder. I hooked it onto the windowsill and unfurled the rope until it reached the grass below. Robin climbed onto the top rung and said, "Hair is on the outside. Character is on the inside."

I simply stood there, on the verge of tears.

"Think about it," she said. "It's what you do best."

Then she was gone.

THE MOST POPULAR GUY
AT SCHOOL

The McFactory felt very empty without Robin. Echo hopped back out of her cage and rested on the windowsill, looking longingly at a flock of wild parrots gathered in our elm tree. And I sat at the lab table wondering if Robin and I would ever see each other again. Or talk again. Or ever hold hands again. I realized that the one-eyed man would not be able to see Echo's pooping spell on the video because it happened in the dark, after the lightning bolt illuminated the lab and scared the poop out of Echo. Those crooks would try to duplicate the formula, but would never get it right. The thought of that cheered me up a little.

I cut a small slice of cucumber and took it to Echo. "Good work today, pal. You really came through."

"Thanks, Matey," she said, taking the cucumber with her right foot. (Most parrots are left-"handed.")

"I'll think of a proper gift for you. Something really special."

I climbed down the rope ladder, went into the house and telephoned the police. I told them everything that had happened and gave them the license plate number of the limo, which was photographed by my infrared periscope camera attached to our chimney. For further evidence, I told them that my McCorder, which I had switched on inside the limousine, covertly captured every word of the whole event.

I went to the new hotel under construction. The workmen allowed me to get the backpacks from the roof.

I walked to school alone. On my way, I saw some of the bald men I'd treated the night before. Whereas Buckholtz's and my hair growth only remained a few hours, on men who were older, the formula lasted longer! Age mattered. That was a breakthrough observation in my research. These men now had full heads of hair. Red hair! They were thrilled. It made me feel good that my product brought so much joy to so many.

Taylor Samuel, the mail carrier, had a thick head of red hair, slicked back. Alan Robison, the gardener, had a new red Afro. Dennis Wallis, Dad's auto mechanic, had gotten rid of his bad toupee and was showing off his new, wavy hairdo. Bubba Oliver, the pier fisherman, loved his red Mohawk. David Stefan, the manager of Burger City, was flaunting dreadlocks. Ironically, with one hundred thousand new hair strands on his head, the plumber Bobby Glenn chose a buzz cut. Bill Kerby, a paramedic, was brushing his page-boy. Homeless Hubert sported a mullet. Officer Hernandez proudly wore a crew cut. All of them waved to me, pumping their fists in the air, grateful to have hair again. It was quite a sight: a whole town of male redheads. Finally, a place I fit right in.

At school, in the library, I found Robin studying by herself at a corner table. I approached her. "Thought you might need your homework," I said, handing over her backpack.

"Thanks," she said quietly.

I took a seat across from her. We sat there. Just the two of us. Saying nothing. Finally, I whispered, "All those offers—they're waiting for a decision."

"Not my decision," Robin said.

"We would split billions of dollars."

"You'll have twice as much without me."

She wasn't going to change her mind, but at least she was talking to me. Kind of.

"The heartbeat of the blue-throated hummingbird has been measured at over one thousand beats per minute," I said.

"Really? The hummingbird thing again?" She rose, took a Gala apple out of her backpack, and said, "For your next science project, remember this: an apple floats because twenty-five percent of its volume is air."

"Seventy-five hundred varieties of apples are grown throughout the world," I responded.

Robin grinned, took a big bite of her apple and left.

That apple fact? Things that float? Swapping trivia. I think it was her way of saying she didn't hate me.

On my way to Social Studies class, three students and one teacher asked for my autograph. Richard Kendall stopped me. "You cured my uncle Seth yesterday. Aunt Paula says he's a new man. Thank you, Morgan. Thank you." Then Richard took a step closer to me and said in quiet tones, "I could use some hair on my chest. Do you think—"

"I'll see what I can do," I said.

After school, I was suddenly everyone's best friend. Charlie Corwin, the most popular kid in Carlsbad, threw his arm around my neck and invited me to a sleepover at his beach house that weekend. Colleen Kaner, voted Homecoming Queen, asked if I would consider going to the Valentine's Day dance with her. The Valentine's Day dance? I had never been to any kind of dance before, much less one with a queen. Hannah Neven (Both her names are palindromes—words that read the same backward as forward) suggested that we start studying together. Robert Foster insisted that I wear his letterman's jacket. And Brad Buckholtz with his two kiss-butt buddies walked up to me.

"Can I talk to you?" Buckholtz asked tentatively.

"Can I talk to you, who?" I said, taking advantage of my new power.

"Morgan. Can I talk to you, Morgan?"

"Yes. You may speak to me, son," I said. "Proceed."

"Here's the hundred dollars I owe you," he said, handing me a wad of cash. "I know your invention is going to make you very rich, but a hundred dollars is a hundred dollars and a deal is a deal. Besides, if I didn't pay up I didn't know what else you'd do to me."

"See what it feels like to be bullied?" I gently pushed his hand away. "Keep your money. But also keep your promise not to harass me. Or anybody else," I said. "Character. It's all about character, Brad."

On my walk home, I called the *Carlsbad Courier* and all the television and radio stations in town informing them that the inventor of *Hair Today*, the phenomenal cure to baldness, had a major announcement to make and would hold a press conference on his front porch at precisely six o'clock that night.

FOLLOWING YOUR HEART IS THE BEST THING

Poppy was watering the front lawn when I got home. His red mustache was still intact. "I'm glad to see you! The phone's been ringing off the hook," he said.

"Who called?"

"About a hundred more financiers who want to invest in *Hair Today*. Plus calls from agents, lawyers, publicists, managers, accountants, bodyguards, even a big Hollywood producer, who wants to make a movie about your life. They all want a piece of you."

"That's insane."

"I got another call, too."

"Oh, yeah? From who?"

Poppy turned off the water. "The police," he said.

"Really? What piece of me did they want?" I asked worriedly.

"They said they caught and arrested some kidnappers."

"Oh." I was barely able to contain my relief.

"What's that all about?" Poppy asked.

I looked at Poppy. Why worry everybody? "It's trivial," I said. After all, nobody got hurt. I was alive. I had my formula. "It's insignificant." I'd tell everyone about the one-eyed man incident later. "It's minor." Now was my time to enjoy being the town hero. "It's nothing important."

Poppy wasn't buying it. "It sounded important, Sparky. What happened?"

"I'd rather not say."

"Why not?"

"A wise, old Irishman once told me: *Today is the yesterday you worry about tomorrow.*"

Poppy smiled and wrapped up the hose. "Well, you're fine. That's all that really matters."

"Thanks," I said. "Thanks for everything."

Poppy dusted himself off. "I told all those money folks from this morning that you would call them back with your decision."

"What did they say?"

"The more I put them off, the more they increased their offers. One included your own island."

"Wow," I said. "How do I decide which offer is best?"

Poppy thought for a moment. "Some wise, old Irishman once said—"

I turned on my McCorder, ready to save and savor Poppy's quote. He continued, *"Follow your heart. It will always lead you down the right path."*

The sun was casting a golden light on our cul-de-sac. One of the six o'clock news crews had some trouble setting up their satellite truck, so my dad helped them solve their technical problems. He knew everything about uplinks, encoders, fiber optics, microwave transmitters, and parabolic antennas. The newspaper journalists waited patiently for all the radio microphones to be put in place.

I was in the bathroom shaving. I looked into the mirror. I saw my red hair, my red freckles, and my red stubble. Shaving was, like Poppy said, time well spent. It gave me a chance to reflect on all that had happened. And all that it meant. I wanted to be able to look myself in the mirror and know that what I was about to do was the right thing. I would have to live with this decision for the rest of my life.

I wanted the movie about me to have a happy ending.

In our living room, Mom straightened my collar just before I went outside to face the press. "You look very handsome, Mr. McCracken," she said. "What are you going to say out there?"

"I'm not exactly sure."

"You'll think of something. You always do."

"Mom," I said. "Do you like Poppy's mustache?"

"I like Poppy. With or without a mustache."

I stepped out onto the front porch. I was looking at a sea of broadcasters and journalists and news equipment. All of our neighbors were standing there, too. Sadly, Robin wasn't among them. I tried to relax with the thought that the standard lead pencil can draw a line thirty-five miles long.

Chloe took me aside. I was hoping she would calm me down with some sage "big sister" advice. She faced me and said, "How do I look?"

She was constantly worried about the way she looked, always fussing with her makeup, her nails, her wardrobe, and her hair, just so people would notice her, would like her. It got me to thinking. She had no idea what I meant when all I said was, "It doesn't matter how you look."

Poppy and Mom made room for Dad, who joined the rest of us on the front porch.

"I've got some *breaking news* of my own," Dad said. "Those guys over there from Channel 5, at the satellite truck, just offered me a job." Dad and Mom hugged. Chloe and I let out a *whoop*. Poppy gave Dad the thumbs up. (Did you know that your thumb is as long as your nose? Or that your forearm is as long as your foot?)

One of the local TV news reporters called out, "It's six o'clock, Morgan. We're live on the air."

I walked behind the row of microphones, cleared my throat and looked out over the crowd. Everybody was just waiting for me to say something. But I didn't know what to say. I was very confused. So, I took a deep breath and let my noggin take over. "Hello. My name is Morgan McCracken. You can call me Morgan."

I hoped nobody could see (or hear) that my knees were knocking together. To relax myself, I offered the crowd a couple nutty facts. "One in three dog owners say they have talked to their pets on the phone. The weight of all the ants in the world is more than the weight of all the people in the world."

There was silence. I tried to start again, "The . . . the . . . the . . ." But, I was still too nervous, so I unleashed another fact. "The word 'the' is the most written and spoken word in the English language." I smiled.

I took another deep breath. Then, thankfully, the words came to me, "I've learned a lot over the last few weeks," I started. "I learned from a wise, old Irishman that time is something you never get back. So, I won't take much more of yours this evening."

I looked at my family for support. Poppy smiled. Mom and Dad nodded. Chloe was applying lipstick.

"I tried to invent a product that would save time—a solution to shaving. Instead, I stumbled on the cure to balding. A friend of mine, well, a partner. I mean a former friend, an ex-partner—uh, let's just say a fuzz-finding neighbor of mine taught me something else about hair. That it's *only* hair. That we shouldn't spend time worrying about it."

I looked up to Robin's window. Her curtains were drawn.

"To all of you bald guys, well, to *everybody*, it doesn't matter if you're fat or thin, short or tall, have big ears or little ears, have a high voice or a low one, or a mole or a limp. It doesn't matter if you have hair on your head or don't have hair on your chest. What matters is being a person who doesn't waste time caring about those things. Because time," I took another deep breath and said, "is something you never get back." Poppy blew his nose into a handkerchief.

Even I couldn't believe what I was about to do next. I took out the scrap of paper on which Robin wrote down the *Hair Today* formula. I held it up.

"Here's the formula to curing baldness. No other copy exists. I've decided not to make any more *Hair Today* or to patent it or to sell it. I've decided to spend time working on other inventions. I've also decided that shaving is a good thing, that being bald isn't a bad thing, and that following your heart is the best thing."

There was stunned silence, as I struck a match and set the note-paper on fire. "Thank you for your time," I said.

At first, nobody spoke or moved. Then, one person—Chloe—started to applaud. Shortly after, another person then another joined her. Before long, everyone was clapping and cheering.

I didn't know how to respond, so I just hugged my parents as bald men around the world probably cursed me, as my greatest invention went up in smoke, as the embers of my beloved formula floated high into the evening sky, past Robin's dark window.

SPREAD YOUR WINGS AND FLY

After cleaning the dinner dishes, I sat on a stool on the back porch as Poppy gave me my monthly haircut. With each snip, I watched my red locks fall to the floor. I looked at the hair and wondered why the world made such a fuss over it. It was just hair.

"Will you miss your mustache when the formula wears off, Poppy?"

"Nah. It's been fun. But I keep thinking there's a whisk broom under my nose."

I let out a deep sigh. It had been a long, long day.

Poppy could tell that I was feeling down. "Having second thoughts?" he asked. "Walking away from fame and fortune isn't easy. Takes a lot of guts."

"I wonder if I did the right thing."

"If it feels right, then you know you did right."

"I lost a friend. That doesn't feel right."

"If she's a true friend, she'll be back."

We shared a moment of quiet, and then I asked, "Do *you* think I did the right thing?"

"A wise, old Irishman has this to say—yes!"

"I just did what you taught me, Poppy. We're McCrackens. We use our noggins to solve our problems."

Poppy trimmed around my ear with his electric clippers. "So what's your next project gonna be?" he asked.

I thought for a moment. "I'd like to learn how to fly."

"Do you want to be a pilot?"

"No. I mean fly without an airplane."

Poppy stopped cutting my hair. His clippers froze in midair. He wasn't afraid of the impossible, so he said, "Flying's the easy part. But make sure you learn how to land first!" We both laughed. He handed me a mirror to examine his work.

"Great haircut. Great advice. Great job, Poppy," I said.

He looked at me and smiled. "You just gave me an idea."

"What?"

"First thing tomorrow morning, I'm going downtown to volunteer at the homeless shelter. I bet they could use a cutterologist!"

"That's using your noggin!"

We high-fived each other.

Later that night, I called a Family Summit. Everyone sat in the living room. On the coffee table I had placed Echo's cage, with Echo dancing around inside. I started my speech. "It's been an interesting day."

"You can say that again!" Chloe said.

"You can say that again!" Echo repeated.

We all laughed. "I wanted to thank you for all your help. I also wanted to ask your permission for something," I said.

"What?" Mom asked.

"When I bought Echo with my own allowance, you said she was mine as long as I fed her and cleaned her cage. Well, after today's events—after she saved my formula—after a lot of thought, I feel she deserves a special reward."

"What kind of reward?" Dad asked.

"Well, I know what it feels like to be in the *McFactory* all day. I realize I've got to get out more. Get off my bony butt more."

Chloe giggled.

"And I think . . ." I looked into Echo's feathery face, "it's time you get out and see the world."

"See the world," Echo joyfully trilled.

Echo nibbled on my finger as I said to her, "You need to be in the sky, in the trees, hanging out with your own kind, meeting a nice mate, settling down, having kids, having grandparrots."

"Aye, aye, aye," Echo said.

"So, may I let Echo fly away?" I asked my family.

"Most household pets can't survive in the wild," Dad said.

"That's true. But parrots can. Happily," I said. "I researched it. Flocks of wild parrots live in many US cities, including New York, San Francisco, and right here in our own backyard. She'll never be further than a squawk away."

"I think it's a lovely idea," Mom said.

"Yeah, it's good to spread your wings and fly," Poppy said, with a wink.

"Chloe. What do you say?"

Chloe thought for a moment and said, "Bye-bye, birdie."

There was a full moon out. (Footprints left on the moon by Apollo astronauts will remain visible for at least ten million years because there is no erosion on the moon.) I knelt in the street, at the end of the cul-de-sac. I was just about to open the little door to Echo's cage when a shadow crossed over me.

"I saw your press conference on TV," said Robin's velvety voice.

"How was my hair?" I asked without turning around. Before she got mad, I added, "I'm kidding!"

"What are you doing?" she asked.

"I had a little talk with Echo."

"About her potty habits?"

"About her freedom."

"What do you mean?"

"I think the secret ingredient should fly away, like a robin. Then nobody, including me, can ever be tempted to make the formula."

"What if Echo is captured? What if she rattles off the formula to some stranger? What if her babies have the same magic poop? What if—"

"Robin?"

"What?"

"I'm out of the hair business. What Echo does with the formula, well, I don't give a poop."

We looked at each other. Finally, she said, "Why did you change your mind?"

"I didn't. You did."

She took a step closer to me.

"So you're letting Echo loose?" Robin said.

"Birds were born to fly. Not to be cooped up in a cage."

I opened Echo's little door. "C'mon, girl," I said. Echo hopped onto my finger and I brought her out into the night air. She looked up, down, and all around. This would be her new world.

I gave her a little peck on top of her head and said, "Go." ("Go" is one of the shortest sentences in the English language.)

"Have fun, Echo," Robin said.

"Aye, aye!" Echo squealed.

And with that, she flapped her wings, flew up and above Crestview Drive, and was soon enveloped by the night sky.

When she was out of sight, a motorcycle cop rode down our street. It was Officer Hernandez. He pulled to a stop beside us, but left his engine running.

"Are you kids okay? It's getting late," he said.

"We're fine," I replied.

He removed his helmet. He was completely bald. "All gone," he said, rubbing his shiny head.

"I'm sorry, Officer Hernandez," I said.

"It's more natural like this. It's the way it supposed to be. I think you helped a lot of us to realize that."

"Thanks," I said. "That means a lot to me."

He put his helmet back on. "You kids take care," he said. Then he roared off into the dark.

When we could no longer hear his motorcycle, Robin turned to me. "Now do you think you made the right decision?"

"Yes."

"Are you still sad about giving up your formula?"

"Yes."

"Will you miss Echo?"

"Yes."

"Do I ask too many questions?"

"Yes."

"Do you have any for me?"

"Yes."

"What?"

I gathered all my strength. All my courage. And took a chance. "Would a girl like you go with a boy like me to an event like the Valentine's Day dance?"

Even though English has over a million words (more than any other language), Robin's answer came without words.

She kissed me.

On my lips.

For just a second.

There are 86,400 seconds in a day. I had lived through 410 hundred million seconds. That kiss was the greatest single second of my life.

Whoever invented kissing deserved the Olympic Gold Medal, the Pulitzer Prize, and the Academy Award.

Robin smiled. I smiled. And we heard a familiar voice from above shriek, "Poop!" We both ducked. But it was too late.

I'm different. You're different. Everyone is different. That's what makes life so interesting. It would be boring if we were all the same.

There's something else that makes life interesting: about a third of all people flush the toilet when they're still sitting on it, which is a Morgan McFactoid way of saying . . .

THE END